Dáil Mhic Cárthaigh
Corcaigh 13/3/95

Ger Philpott was born in Cork in 1957. He taught for ten years in Ireland, the Caribbean and the US. His short film *Change* was the dual winner of the Arts Council and Film Base/RTE Short Script Awards in 1994. He lives in Dublin and works as a writer and film maker.

DEEP END

DEEP END

GER PHILPOTT

POOLBEG

Published in 1995 by
Poolbeg Press Ltd,
Knocksedan House,
123 Baldoyle Industrial Estate,
Dublin 13, Ireland

A catalogue record for this book is available from the British Library.

ISBN 1 85371 442 9

Cover photograph courtesy of JWT
Cover design by Poolbeg Group Services Ltd
Set by Poolbeg Group Services Ltd in Garamond 10.5/13.5
Printed by The Guernsey Press Ltd,
Vale, Guernsey, Channel Islands.

I wish to acknowledge:

The support of my family and friends. AIDSWISE and the assistance of *The Irish Times* library staff and Tony Heffernan, Democratic Left. The valuable guidance and friendship of my editor, Kate Cruise O'Brien. The team at Poolbeg for publishing *Deep End*. And above all those amongst whom I am blessed, they know who they are. Thank you.

For
Mary, Tadhg, Patsy

and
Brian

The library was on the Mardyke. Posher than the City Library which was downtown on Grand Parade. I went there one day with my elder brother, Ted. It was a week day, we were off school. He didn't like hanging out with his younger brother. We walked up the North Mall and crossed the river Lee on Vincent's Bridge. We called it the "rusty bridge". A pedestrian bridge that spanned the river at the Irish Distiller's gate. It got its name from the colour of the *Lowe Rust* paint it was caked in. An over-sized meccano bridge. With high wide sides.

I bet you're afraid to walk across the top, Ted said.

He was right. But I'd show him.

If you can do it I can do it, I replied.

I climbed up after him and walked across the flat metal-studded girder. It was freezing and I was scared. I was chuffed when we reached the other side.

We spent about an hour in the library.

It's snowing, Ted told me as we browsed through the shelves. Hurry up!

Snow was falling heavily when we got outside. The light was blinding. Nobody on the streets. We had a snowball fight as we made our way home.

I've never seen snow on the ground like this before, I said.

I have, Ted said.

I didn't believe him. After all he was only three years

older than me. A few cars drove by, making slush of the snow on the roads.

Hurry up we'll be late for our lunch, he said as I dilly-dallied in the snow.

I'm coming, I said as I rushed to catch up with him. I skidded in the snow.

Wow. Look at that, I said as I crossed over the road to the "rusty bridge".

What? Ted asked.

There aren't any footprints in the snow.

I was so excited as we walked across the undisturbed snow covered bridge.

This is the best day of my life, I said.

Why? Ted asked.

Because it's like the first time the bridge has ever been crossed, I replied.

We walked on. Slowly.

I'll never forget this day, I said. Why did we get the day off school?

For your man's funeral, Ted answered.

Wasn't he buried before now?

Not in a grave.

Where so?

In a lime pit, he replied.

What's that?

I don't know, he said.

What's his name anyway?

Roger Casement, he said.

I'm glad they brought his body back, I thought.

Chapter One

28 - 12 - 82

Dear Ger,

Sorry no festive communications but I have been off the rails in hospital for the past three weeks. They have let me out for Xmas.

I am staying in the mews. I have Hodgkins disease which is a bit nasty but I will be better in a couple of months. On 18 tablets a day, chemotherapy, and radiation. So, feeling lousy at the moment. The itch I had all summer was part of the symptoms! And I'm still itching.

Hoping you had a wild Christmas – Give me a shout, or a ring, before you go skiing. Excuse letter and writing as I am a bit high on tablets.

Regards to all in Cork.

Love to you

R. Paul.

I'm going to the shop, I called upstairs as I pulled the front door shut behind me.

The postman cycled towards me. I collected our post from him when I met him at the corner of the road. It was a watery, sunny January morning. I walked along the Cross Douglas Road towards the Back Douglas Road.

When I was a kid I thought these roads were named to help the confused residents who lived on them. I sorted the letters as I went to the local shop to buy milk for breakfast. I opened the envelope. The letter was from my partner Paul. I was in Cork to help some friends decorate their new house. My relationship with Paul was in trouble. And I opted for some time out.

What did it mean? Was he going to live? Was he going to die? Cancer is serious stuff. How did I feel about him? How did I feel about myself? My stomach spun as I grappled with the contents of the letter. I wanted to be a little boy again and not need to know what to do. I stopped outside the telephone box, near the shop, on my way back to the house. Ring him, I thought. But I couldn't.

I was angry with him because I hadn't heard from him since he visited me the previous November. He'd been working in Blarney, outside Cork, for a day. He called to know if I wanted anything brought down from Dublin. We arranged to meet late on a Thursday night in Hills Bar on McCurtain Street. It was Cork's only gay bar. Cork still only has one gay bar. A gay guide book would have described Hills as fifty-fifty. Meaning it was mixed. I told Paul that I didn't want to deal with the pressure if he stayed with me. So he booked into the Metropole Hotel, also on McCurtain Street. I was still angry about his sleeping around.

I sat in the pub waiting for him on that wet miserable night. I was early and he was late. I remembered the row which led to my flight to Cork. It was about two postcards he'd sent from Spain. He'd taken a holiday there with a friend the previous September. I didn't want him to go away. But he did. He sent me the proverbial scenic card.

Denny, his brother, got an entirely different one. It showed an arty shot of a cave opening. And the caption read, *This is one of the many interesting orifices I'm exploring while here. Doing my utmost to explore all before my return.*

I was furious when I saw the card in Denny's flat. I left for Cork two days after Paul returned from holiday.

I made a mental note, as I sat in the bar waiting for Paul, never to be early for a meeting like this. I saw him cross the street dodging between traffic. Yet again I was struck by how handsome he was.

Sorry I'm late, he said smiling. He still had the grey look about him I'd first noticed when he came back from Spain.

How was the trip down? I asked.

The traffic was crazy, he replied.

What would you like to drink ? I asked.

A pint of lager, he answered.

I went to the bar and ordered drinks. I watched his reflection in the silkscreen patterned mirrors behind the bar. He seemed listless. I put it down to the tiring journey from Dublin.

Have you eaten? he asked when I came back from the bar.

Yes. Have you?

No. I had a sandwich before I left, he said.

We spent the rest of the evening drinking and talking.

Will you stay with me in the hotel? he asked as time was called.

I don't know . . . Why not? I said, a pregnant pause later.

There was something wholly seedy about being in the hotel. It was a grand swirly-carpet-type hotel. I felt embarrassed as we walked into the foyer. We'd decided to be nonchalant about it. Just in case anyone asked whether I was a resident. *Just* one of the coping skills gay people have to develop! We rekindled lost passions. Sort of. The hangover the next morning wasn't much better.

★ ★ ★

I called Paul when I got back from the shop with the milk. He didn't answer. I reread the letter. I was amused that he referred to his itching the previous Summer. I wondered if he meant this as a metaphor for the difficulty our relationship was in?

I'm going to be fine, Paul said when I eventually spoke to him.

Are you sure?

With plenty of rest and proper medical attention, I'll be right as rain in no time, he reassured me.

He'd been diagnosed with Hodgkin's disease. Cancer of the lymphatic system. I spoke with a friend's brother – a medical student – later that day and found out that this type of cancer has four distinct stages. Its prognosis depended on when it was first diagnosed. This wasn't a problem. Of course it was caught at the right stage, I told myself. Why wouldn't it be? Paul came from a medical family. Everything was bound to be okay.

I'll come and visit at the weekend, I told him.

★ ★ ★

I remembered the row we had when I'd first found out about his philandering. I wish you'd die of cancer, I shouted at Paul. It seemed like a good weapon at the

6

time. I felt bad about it then. But the feeling distracted me from thinking about his illness. I was annoyed that he got sick. Part of me felt it would gloss over our troubled relationship. Without properly sorting things out.

* * *

I travelled to Dublin a few days after getting the letter. I wondered about whether it'd be okay to have sex with Paul now that he had cancer. I thought this as the train's brakes ground to a halt in Limerick Junction, the armpit of Ireland. Sex wasn't on the agenda that weekend. Paul was grumpy and tetchy.

I'm pissed off with you for only visiting because I'm sick, he told me.

You only wrote to me when you were sick, I retorted. Then I shut up. I didn't know *what* to say.

I tried to work out how I felt about Paul. Yes, I still loved him but I wasn't convinced that getting back together with him was the right thing to do. He was staying with his mother while he got better. So a decision about moving back to Dublin wouldn't have to be made straight away.

I've been asked to go to the US via the Far East with some friends and their baby boy, I told Paul.

When were you asked?

Over Christmas, I answered.

How long would you be gone for? he asked.

About four months. We're leaving in May, I answered.

So you're going?

I nodded as I looked at him.

Unlucky in love but nothing a suntan wouldn't sort out, I remember thinking flippantly when I was asked to go on the trip. I'd just taken a degree in economics and sociology at University College Cork. It was 1982. The world was my oyster. And I was naive. Sometimes – I wish I was still. But only sometimes.

* * *

Paul and I met for the first time in a bar in Cork in 1979. It was a Saturday night. I'd spent the afternoon playing tennis with a girlfriend just outside Cork. We had a few drinks on the way back to the city.

Let's call into Hills, Margaret, my companion, said as we drove along the quayside. The estuary was at full tide. We parked on McCurtain Street opposite the pub. We smoked a joint in the car. We could see the crowd in the bar through its large tinted glass window. We got out of the car. We laughed as we walked to the bar.

Hello, how are you? he asked immediately I walked through the door.

He had intelligent blue eyes. He face was striking. A strong nose, clear skin and a great head of curly brown hair.

Couldn't be better I replied, cockily.

Are you sure? he asked, smirking.

Arrogant git, I thought, smiling.

The usual? Margaret asked as she went to the bar. I nodded.

The bar was always full on Saturday nights. We stood very close to each other. It was a bit disconcerting but not unenjoyable. He's about the same height as me, I thought as we stared at each other. It was clear what our intentions were. His charisma was powerful. Adrenalin coursed through my body. He made me feel like the most important person in the universe – okay – the bar. The juke-box belted out song after song and the crowded bar faded into oblivion.

I was normally socially adroit but found that I was adrift in his company. I was spellbound. Even with the fortifying effect of marijuana I found the encounter challenging.

Would you describe yourself as clever? he asked.

We looked at each other. Me with raised eyebrows and a grimace. He with a mock serious expression. We laughed. Our laughter hit a chord and I knew that something significant was afoot. He wore a viyella shirt and cord trousers. I thought this was a bit naff, dressed as I was in American-retro. My gear was the trophy of a Summer spent in New York *exploring my sexuality* far away from Cork. His sex appeal more than compensated for his tweediness.

He's got the social graces down to a fine art, I thought as I excused myself and went to the toilet. I rolled a joint in the cubicle. When I came out of the cubicle he was waiting for me. It wasn't a very big toilet and we were alone.

So that's what you were up to, he said.

I smiled.

He leaned against the door blocking access in – or out. He took a lighter from his pocket. He lit the joint and we smoked it. He caressed my neck. Just behind my ear. I looked at him. And then we kissed. He kissed well.

Would you like to spend the night? he asked.

Yes, I answered. Take it easy, the voice in my head said. I opted to play cool.

But I have family commitments tomorrow, I said.

Call me in Dublin soon, he said, as we left the bar.

9

I don't have your number, I replied, smiling enigmatically.

It's in the book – if you're interested, he said.

If you're interested.

* * *

The first of a series of messages from Paul arrived a few weeks later. He sent cards, brief letters and he left a telephone message. They all came to me c/o the bar in McCurtain Street. I let on that I was blase. But I was thrilled. One day a card arrived which simply said *Change a little and a lot can happen. Tingle. Tingle. R. Paul.*

I called eventually and agreed to visit him in Dublin for a weekend.

I travelled with a friend – Sean – who was also to spend his first weekend with a new boyfriend. I hitched to the roundabout at Dunkettle bridge, on the N8, at six thirty to meet Sean the Friday morning we left. Sean was the same age as Paul, five years my senior. We'd had a stormy friendship. He was renowned for his sarcasm and had been very rude to me from time to time.

You trumped me one evening, at a party, while I was in full flight, he told me as we drove through the countryside. That changed my opinion of you, he said.

We made it to Dublin in record time in his X-19 sports car. Sean described how he'd met his boyfriend, what he was like and his anticipation of the weekend ahead.

Tell me about Paul? he asked.

He's drop-dead sexy, I said.

And? he said.

But there wasn't much more that I could say. And I thought that I must've been mad to go on this trip. I realised that I'd spent approximately three hours in this stranger's company and now I was going to spend a weekend with him.

I remember him the night you met in the bar, Sean said, I didn't realise that you liked older men.

That explained why you never noticed I had a crush on you for all those years, I thought.

Sean dropped me off at the Kilkenny Design Centre, on Nassau Street. He was a designer and had a meeting to go to. It was 9.15 on Friday morning. I bought *The Irish Times* and headed for Bewley's on Grafton Street. Paul wouldn't be home from work until early evening – he was an agricultural advisor and was down the country with a client. I wandered around the bookshops and clothes shops and went to the National Gallery for the afternoon. I was getting more nervous as the hours passed.

The plan was that I'd leave a message of my whereabouts on Paul's answerphone. I went to Rice's bar on Stephen's Green – Ireland's oldest gay bar – around 5.00pm. I sat in the straight part of the bar. I called Paul shortly after 6.00pm. I remember the Angelus on the pub's television.

Where are you? he asked.

I'm in Rice's, I said.

He laughed.

You don't waste much time, he teased.

I've been in Dublin since early morning, I explained.

I'll be there in half-an-hour, Paul said.

I ordered more coffee and read as I waited. The door of the pub swung open and an old couple carrying their shopping walked in, Paul was behind them. We smiled at each other as the couple shifted towards a table. Paul came over and kissed me on the cheek. How cosmopolitan, I thought. He took my bag and we left immediately.

Let's go to my house. Drop off the bags and go out for dinner, he suggested.

Sounds great, I said nodding.

I had no knowledge of Dublin's geography apart from downtown. We drove towards Rathmines and crossed the bridge turning on to the canal. I noticed some mallards on the canal as we turned right on to Mount Pleasant Avenue. The houses were Victorian. We stopped outside number 9.

The door was painted matt grey. We went inside as Paul saluted some neighbours. The house was painted white and had a patterned runner on the grey carpeted hall-way. An old mahogany blanket chest stood to the left. A plain cutlery box, with a large turquoise vase to its right, sat on top. A gilded mirror hung over it. A tapestry-seated prie-dieu stood under an archway at the bottom of the stairs. An oriental silk wall hanging draped the first flight of stairs.

We walked to the end of the hallway, down some stairs towards the kitchen. A dark bentwood coat-stand stood to the left of the half glass swing door. We kissed in the kitchen. Paul gave me a guided tour of the house. I shied at the bedroom.

Would you like to have a bath? Paul suggested. He sensed my nervousness.

I jumped at the opportunity. At least I'd have some time to myself, I thought. I'd also be able to figure out how I'd handle the situation.

Paul gave me a towel. A small towel. I went to the bedroom to change. I heard the sound of the bath water running.

Do you like Badedas? Paul shouted from the bathroom.

Sure, I love it, I answered.

A large glass and mahogany bookcase stood at one

end of the bedroom. A tallboy stood between the two large windows opposite the large bed. I could see the verdigrised dome of Rathmines church through the window nearest the fireplace. A stripped pine (window shutters joined together) wardrobe occupied the alcove to the right of the fireplace, the other housed a sink with more stripped shutters for cupboard doors underneath. There was a bedside locker on one side and a table on the other side of the biggest bed I'd ever seen.

It belonged, the frame at least, to a Lord Londonderry, Paul said. A carver chair stood against the connecting door to the back bedroom. I undressed slowly, reading the book titles.

Lots of Lawrence and Forster amidst an otherwise eclectic collection. When I thought that the bath was ready I went down to the bathroom on the half-landing. The bathroom was full of steam as I opened the door. I was shocked to find Paul in the bath. I dropped my towel and I climbed in to join him. I was dying with embarrassment.

When I saw how nervous you were I felt that the best thing was to jump in at the deep end, he said later.

Things didn't happen after that Badedas bath. I was rigid with nerves. Indeed my nerves were the only part of me that were rigid. We lay in bed talking for hours and ate in a neighbourhood joint in Rathmines Shopping Centre around midnight. We slept holding each other.

Sex is off the agenda until you're comfortable, Paul whispered in my ear.

Relieved, I cursed my flagging manhood. We got up early next morning and went to Bewley's for breakfast. Then we strolled around town.

We have a cottage in Wicklow. Would you like to go there for lunch? Paul asked.

13

I'd love to, I said.

We picked up some things at McCambridges in Ranelagh en route. Soup. Bread. Cheese. Cabonosi. Pate. Cake.

I hope you haven't charged these to my account, barked an old woman who was watching us as Paul took the packages from the man behind the counter.

Hello mother, Paul said turning. This is my friend, Ger from Cork, he said. This is my mother, Barbara.

Hello, I said and smiled. Paul had charged the food to her account.

* * *

The drive to Glenbride in Wicklow was enjoyable as we sang along to Diana Ross's *Do you know where you're going to?* How appropriate, I thought of the disastrous sex the night before. We turned off the main road on to a lesser, bumpy road that climbed the side of a mountain.

We couldn't find a suitable old cottage in this area, Paul explained, so we bought a derelict cottage on this site, knocked it down and built this cottage from scratch.

The cottage was situated impressively halfway up its steep hilly site. A winding driveway, cut between two large embankments, led to the cottage itself. The views overlooking the farmhouses below, to the mountains on the other side of the valley, were magnificent. A Shangri-La.

We went for a long walk up the mountain behind the cottage. I was determined that we'd have sex and this cottage seemed as good a place as any. We made love on the mountain. The earth didn't move. We stopped at a country pub for a few pints of Guinness on the way back to Dublin. I was feeling much more relaxed and that evening we made love again. The sex was getting better.

Paul was an incredibly passionate man. It seems strange, even now, to describe him in the past tense. You couldn't but be aware of his presence. Even still, eleven years later, I frequently register a sense of longing – a surge of feeling in my gut – that can never be satisfied. Teachers in school used to say that it's easier to stay warm on a cold day if you expand rather than huddle yourself together.

* * *

I moved unofficially to Dublin. My only tie with Cork was the fact that I had to finish my studies. I didn't know what I wanted to do with my life. I'd gone to University so as not to have to go to work. While there, I discovered sex-drugs-rock'n'roll. And now I was in love. Paul was worried that I'd get bored during the Summer. But I did a number of jobs, organising auctions, catering, gardening, but mostly painting and decorating. I kept busy.

I may have been uncertain about a career path but there was no doubt about my desire to pay my own way. The Summer was good. I enjoyed work and relished the thought that next year, for the first time in my life, there wouldn't be any exams. The ultimate liberation. I was young and my attitudes completely outstripped my experience.

I moved to Dublin formally the following Summer, after my exams. The Summer rolled on. One day I realised that I didn't want to go home. Why? I wasn't sure. Something had happened. Things were different. The Paul I knew had changed or seemed to have changed. I couldn't quite put my finger on it. It had to do with little things. He was short-tempered from time to time. At first with other people, family mainly. Then with me. It was as if someone or something had robbed his zest for life. His enthusiasm waned. He wasn't running on full speed. I couldn't remember when this began, I just knew that it happened.

Paul was as consistently good-humoured as always in public. Privately, he was different. He grew distant and irritable. I found this difficult to deal with.

I know that things have been difficult lately, he said one day. You shouldn't take this personally. It's something wrong with me.

He couldn't pinpoint exactly what he meant by this.

What exactly does this mean? I asked.

I wasn't having any of this crap. Putting pressure on Paul never got results. I had previously admired his thoroughbred air but now it was starting to be a pain in the ass, not to mention being bloody boring. I tried to compensate with little things. But Paul became more and more withdrawn.

My behaviour changed which in turn affected our relationship. My over-anxious attempts to make things better did nothing to alleviate the problems. Stress. Tension. Pain. I felt cheated that he wasn't living up to his end of the bargain – whatever that bargain meant. I thought he was being a spoilt brat and not pulling his weight.

* * *

Paul believed in a golden rule – no one else should know about our arguments. Elaborate performances for the benefit of others and frosty scenes at home. However, I was of the opposite school of thought – if you have a problem let's hear about it. One Saturday evening we were out with some friends for dinner. It had been a glorious sunny day and we'd worked in the garden. Paul was bad-tempered throughout the day. He was his old charming self at the dinner party. This pissed me off no end.

You were very quiet this evening, Paul said on the way home in the car.

I was bored, I replied. And you annoyed me.

How?

You spend the day dumping on me and then charm the socks off everyone at the dinner party.

I wasn't in good form today, that's all, he said.

Yeah. Right, I said slamming the door of the car outside our house.

I stormed into the house and went down the stairs, at the end of the hallway, into the kitchen.

I can't help my mood swings, Paul shouted as he pushed the swing door open and grabbed my hand.

You can bloody well perform for others. So why should I have to deal constantly with your bad temper? I retorted.

He twisted my arm and pushed me against the wall.

You're hurting me, I said as he lifted his other hand to hit me. We stared at each other.

Now I suppose you're going to hit me, will that make you feel better? I shouted, as we struggled.

He released me. I smiled, moral victory won. I wanted him to hit me. That way at least things would've seemed real. I found the intangible tension unbearable. We didn't know what was happening to us. We cried and made love.

My patience was short-lived. I became what he described as difficult. But, though it was tough going at stages, there were many good times that Summer. As things transpired it was to be our last Summer as we knew them. The following Summer – our final Summer – everything had changed. Changed utterly.

Chapter Two

I met Paul's mother again the first weekend I stayed with him in Dublin. Paul and I were ice-skating at the rink in Dolphin's Barn on the Sunday afternoon.

I've got to call into the mother's house for a few minutes, Paul said as we drove away from the ice rink.

We crossed the canal and made our way towards Clonskeagh.

Yes, she's in. Her car's here, Paul said as we drove into the driveway.

I felt apprehensive as we climbed the steps to the house. She hadn't seemed pleased that Paul had charged his purchases to her account when we bumped into her the previous afternoon at the local deli. Paul opened the door with his key.

It's me, Paul called from the hallway. Where are you?

I'm in the dining-room, dear, she answered.

She lived alone. She sat in the redundant dining-room working her way through a stack of papers.

You remember Ger from yesterday, Paul said. She glanced at me over the top of her glasses. Her grey hair was piled behind her head in a bun.

Nice to see you again, I said.

Yes, how was the cottage, dear? she asked as she looked at Paul.

Good. You'll never guess where we've been? Paul said.

Where have you been? she asked with a short laugh.

Ice-skating in Dolphin's barn.

What are you drinking? Paul asked looking at the empty glass on the table.

Hmmm, gin and tonic. Would you care for one?

Yes, thank you, I said.

Fix me one while you're at it. Will you dear? she said. You'll have to make more tonic. And the soda stream is acting up again, she said exasperatedly as Paul walked out of the room.

I'll have a look at it, he said.

Paul returned with the drinks and they discussed some business matters. Tax and things like that. Paul went to the bathroom.

I don't know who you are, young man, but my son appears to be enjoying himself in your company. That's good. He doesn't have enough fun in his life. He works too hard. I trust that what you're hearing remains confidential, after all you are drinking my gin and tonic, she rattled.

Yes, he does seem to be enjoying himself. Very nice gin and tonic it is too, I replied tilting my glass in her direction.

Shall we go? Paul asked as he came back into the room.

Goodbye, I said. Thank you for the drink.

Cheerio, she replied in her clipped tone.

Her bark is worse than her bite, Paul explained in the car on the way home.

A tough nut was my impression.

I'm glad you've met, he said as he squeezed my knee.

* * *

My weekend in Dublin was extended to a long weekend
– a very long weekend. I didn't return to Cork until the
following Wednesday. We slept late each day and Paul
would dash to work mid-morning. I'd drift through the
rest of the day, reading, and wait for him to return from
work. He wined and dined me. Extravagantly.

This is the shortest working week I've ever had, Paul
said one evening over dinner. We both smiled.

Those few days seemed like an eternity. There was
little distinction between them, one flowed into the next. I
didn't want to go back to Cork.

As we continued to see each other, long weekends
became a well-established pattern in our relationship. I
was studying economics and sociology at University
College Cork. Soon I was just making a mid-week return
trip to Cork from Dublin to collect lecture notes from
friends.

There is so much that we have to do, Paul said to me
one Easter weekend when we were sitting in a bar in
Killeagh, Co Cork. I hadn't a clue what he was on about.
What do you mean? I asked.

He looked at me, smiled and said nothing. I've often
wondered if he'd had a sense that his life would be
foreshortened. I didn't know my arse from my elbow about
life, not to mention relationships, then. I was fathoms out of
my depth. It was such an exciting time. And I was
captivated. But I had difficulty working out what I was
feeling. How I was feeling. I was thrilled and terrified by
our lovemaking. Thrilled for obvious reasons. Terrified for
unknown reasons. I'd never been in love. Nothing had
prepared me for this passion. It was heady stuff. All
consuming. I was scared. Yet I felt as if I was ten feet tall.

* * *

Paul came to Cork after my Summer exams. We met for lunch in a friend's restaurant. I had to get Paul off the streets in the afternoon. I couldn't handle his ardour. I fancied myself as a rebel. But Cork's Oliver Plunkett Street on a Saturday afternoon was not the place to make a stance! I cajoled him into The Rob Roy, a bar on Cook's Street. We bonked in the pub's telephone booth. Trying not to fall out of the booth into the bar.

I travelled to Dublin two weeks later to spend my first Summer with Paul. I took a mid-morning Sunday train out of Cork's Kent Station. It got into Dublin's Heuston Station at lunch-time. I'd worked a week of double shifts at my part-time waiter's job to get some money together. And I celebrated my departure from Cork with friends after work the night before. I was badly hungover.

Paul picked me up at the station. Louise, a college class-mate, got on the crowded train at Limerick junction. The journey was shortened by our chat and laughter. We joked about how far away now the exam fever of the previous few weeks seemed, as we drank warm bottles of Heineken. We talked about our romances. Louise was also spending a romantic Summer – in Belfast. We felt important.

Louise spotted Paul first as we made our way slowly along the crowded platform in Dublin. She knew him. They'd met during one of his trips to Cork. She teased me about his clothes. Paul was wearing white jeans and a bright – very bright – yellow shirt. I made a mental note to take him shopping. Again, his confidence shone through.

How are you? I thought you might have changed your mind, he said as he kissed me on the mouth. I felt vulnerable in that public place. Yet safe.

Never, I said.

We walked to the car, got in and kissed again.

What *are* you wearing, Paul? I asked. You look a right mess.

I found these jeans you left behind a few weeks ago and I thought I'd wear them to look younger, Paul explained.

A big mistake, I said as I shook my head. We both broke into laughter.

We spent the afternoon at the beach, making love.

* * *

I developed a penchant for sex alfresco. We'd made love on a beach for the first time the previous Easter in Red Barn, near Youghal in Co Cork. I'd spent most of my childhood Summers in Youghal with my family. Paul and I were visiting friends in Waterford for the weekend and I dragged him off to the beach one morning, before daybreak. I had this burning desire to have sex with him on the beach in Youghal. The tide was low when we got there. So we drove a few miles along the coast until we reached Red Barn. Paul was curious.

What are we doing here? Paul asked.

This is where I spent most of my childhood Summers, I explained. We walked here every day from our house near Green Park in the town, I added.

Paul and I drove past the mobile-home park and the pitch-and-putt club. We parked the car as close to the beach as possible. We climbed over Clay Castle and scrambled onto the beach. The tide never came in too far at this end of the beach and we walked in our bare feet, holding hands.

All of the movies I'd ever seen, from *Love Story* to you-name-it are running through my mind, I said. Fuck you, world, I shouted. This is possible for me too.

We made love in the sand as the dawn broke. We lay in each other's arms as I thought of my childhood, the supermarkets, everywhere that I didn't feel real. Other early morning risers walked on the beach as we pulled on our jeans.

* * *

Paul had bought 9 Mount Pleasant Avenue Lower when it was full of run-down bedsits. He restored it beautifully. The house was his life. It consumed all of his energy and most of his passion. He had marked out different phases for its restoration. He'd also reached a stage in his life when he wanted a relationship. We met soon after he'd made the decision. I began to live with him in the middle of the restoration project.

I loved the house. I felt secure there. My childhood loneliness. The isolation I felt growing up. The difficulty I had dealing with my sexuality all began to make sense there. I'd found someone to love, or rather, he'd found me. The house represented our relationship. It was part of what we were. We made love in every room, on every step of the stairs. It resonated with our passion.

Number 9 has become a much more lived-in place, *a home*, since you've arrived, Paul's older brother told me one day.

I was pleased to hear this. I understood what he

meant. But, I'd no desire to be seen as the happy home-maker.

* * *

There was a lacquered – japanned – cabinet outside the bathroom on the return of the house, just before the spare bedroom. Paul told me the story of the cabinet as we lay beside the cabinet having made love next to it one Sunday afternoon. Our bodies warmed by the sun filtering through the fanlight.

My mother gave it to me for my tenth birthday, he explained.

It was full of little drawers and sections in which he kept an impressive amount of childhood mementoes. Letters he received while he was at boarding school. The contents of these gave the background to his family life. And explained his lonely childhood. Photographs. Baubles of various descriptions.The cabinet was choc-a-bloc. A veritable treasure trove. Soon the floor was covered with its contents. I realised, as the exploration continued, that the cabinet was very important to Paul. He'd stashed the contents there for future reference like a chipmunk saves nuts. As we pieced the jigsaw puzzle of his life together I began to understand him. I loved that cabinet. I asked Paul's younger brother for the cabinet about a year after Paul's death. He told me I could have it, if I paid him fifteen hundred pounds. I still fantasise about having it.

People relied on Paul. He was his mother's favourite son. He had two brothers. I became involved in their family life. His older brother, Andrew was married and lived on the opposite side of Mount Pleasant Avenue. His younger brother, Denny, was also gay and lived in Paul's house with his boyfriend for a time. He was considered unreliable. I was very fond of him and nick-named him the teddybear. I liked all of them.

His mother's constant presence annoyed me. She relied on Paul greatly. He was at her beck and call.

I'm sorry for imposing on you, dear, but you're the only one I can depend on, she said repeatedly.

In her eyes same-sex relationships were not off-bounds as were heterosexual ones. Paul and I would frequently spend the weekends with her at her cottage in Wicklow. I loved the outdoors, working in the garden, climbing the mountain behind the cottage and enjoying the magnificent views. We'd eat and get drunk together. Paul and I would sleep in the only bedroom with a double bed. With her unspoken approval.

★ ★ ★

I'm going for a pint with Patsy this evening, I told Paul that night during supper. We're going to Doheny and Nesbitt's. Would you like to join us?

I'll catch up with you before closing time, Paul said. I've got some paper work to do for tomorrow first.

I walked down the canal towards Leeson Street Bridge and crossed over on to Fitzwilliam Place. I cut across by Fitzwilliam Square and on to Baggot Street. Patsy and I'd planned to meet upstairs in the pub.

Where's Paul? Is he not joining us? Patsy asked as I sat beside her.

He'll get in for last orders, I said.

Patsy and I caught up on the latest scandal and enjoyed a couple of pints of Guinness.

Well, Paul's obviously not going to join us, Patsy said as she went to the bar to get drinks when the barman called last orders.

I guess not, I answered.

We settled into the last pints and bade our goodbyes before heading off to our respective homes. When I got home Paul was asleep. I went to the garage at the end of the garden next morning to collect something. On the way back to the kitchen I noticed that the curtains in the spare bedroom were drawn. This struck me as odd. The room was rarely used. I remembered the curtains were closed as I cleaned my teeth after breakfast.

Hurry up, I'll be late, Paul called from the hallway. He was giving me a lift into town that morning.

Coming, I answered as I went into the spare bedroom, next to the bathroom, and opened the curtains. On my way out of the room I saw that the bedcover was tossed. I straightened it out and noticed a damp patch in the middle. I was shocked. It was obvious that someone had had sex on that bed. Recently.

You're very quiet, Paul said as we drove along the canal. Did you have too much to drink last night?

I was seething.

Nope, I replied. Why did you close the curtains in the spare room last night?

Because it was cold, he said.

How did the stain get on the bedcovers? I asked

What stain?

You know fucking well what stain, I said. You had no intention of joining us in the pub. Had you? Did you call whoever it was up or did he just happen to drop by? I shouted.

I've got to rush, he said as he dropped me off at the

bottom of Merrion Square. We'll talk tonight.

Don't bet on it, I said as I slammed the door.

* * *

My father didn't believe in monogamy. And Denny doesn't believe in it. So why should I, he shouted at me later that evening.

You'd better rethink this if you want me to be around, I retorted. It's not on.

The phone rang.

It's Mother. I have to go around to her house. I'll be back in half-an-hour, he said as he went towards the hall door.

I took a bath. I was gob-smacked. Later, in bed, Paul behaved as if nothing had happened.

Why don't you want to have sex? he asked when I rejected his advances.

Because I think you're a bollocks, I replied.

It took a few weeks before things appeared to get back to normal. But my trust in Paul had been broken. And no matter how attentive his behaviour was, I felt betrayed. I couldn't believe what he said. I subsequently discovered that this episode was only one in a litany of his extra-curricular activities.

* * *

Please don't go? he asked as I walked out of the kitchen. It'll never happen again. I promise you.

Paul had come in to the kitchen from the garden a few moments earlier. He'd been working on restoring an old pianoforte he'd bought.

I'm leaving, I roared at him when he came into the kitchen.

What's wrong? he asked.

I suppose you're going to tell me that I *imagined* what I saw in the garage?

I'd made some coffee and had brought a cup out to the garage at the end of the back garden for Paul. The garage door to the garden locked from the inside. I went to the window, which looked on to the garden, to attract his attention. I saw Paul fucking someone over a barrel.

I didn't leave him. We agreed that I'd not lay any recriminations at his feet. And he would get his act together. The healing process was slow. And difficult. I always felt on the outside when I was a child. I'd found something in my relationship with Paul that I'd never experienced before. Fulfilment. I didn't want to throw that away. My instincts were to walk away from the relationship. But I couldn't. I didn't want to be seen as a failure. Women beaten by their husbands sometimes don't get out. Like them, I stayed and took further abuse. These postcards he sent from Spain, however, ended all hope of things working out. I returned to Cork for a couple of months.

★ ★ ★

Months later I discovered that Paul was sick and began visiting him in Dublin at weekends. I went skiing in Italy that February. I arranged to see Paul on the way and to spend a week with him in Dublin when I came back. We had a good night before I left. We had dinner in town with some friends over a few bottles of wine.

It's really good to see you again, Paul, our dinner companions said. We'll get the bill, they said as the waitress brought the bill.

No, I'll get it, Paul said.

Thank you, I'll take that, I said to the waitress as I picked up the bill.

Are you sure? Paul said as he looked at me across the table.

Yes, I nodded. We looked at each other for a few moments. It was the first time I'd paid for dinner.

We said goodbye to the others and walked along Grafton Street towards the car which was parked on Stephen's Green.

I'd rather not go to the house, he said as we drove off.

Why not, I asked.

It'll be cold. The heating hasn't been on for weeks, he said. We could stay in Clonskeagh?

In the mews? I asked.

No. In the main house, he said.

Do you really not want to go to number nine?

Yes, he answered.

We drove the rest of the way to Clonskeagh in silence and spent the night in Paul's mother's vacant house. She'd recently moved into the attached mews. Paul was frightened to go back to Mount Pleasant Avenue that night. I thought it was because it meant he'd have had to face up to the reality that he had cancer. I didn't know what was going on. We were drunk and made love in his mother's old house. He left in the middle of the night. It was strange.

* * *

What's the definition of a bottom? (the term used to describe the receptive partner in gay sex) asked a friend.

I don't know, I answered.

Whoever gets there first, he replied.

Most people assume that strict roles are adopted by the partners, for sex, in a gay relationship. Lots of gay men pussy-foot around about it too. It's not like that. People are *versatile*. They flip-flop. Paul became the bottom after I moved to Cork.

★ ★ ★

During the trip to Italy I woke from a nightmare one night in tears. I'd dreamt that Paul was in hospital, he was very ill. He didn't look like himself at all. He was upset and agitated. In the dream he died alone, lonely. I tried to make sense of the dream at the time but couldn't. I didn't, or wouldn't, connect it with his disease.

I was full of the joys of Spring when I came back from Italy. I was eager to see Paul and looked forward to spending the following week with him. I'd called him from Italy and arranged to meet him at the house. This was to be the first time we were there together since I went to Cork the previous September.

When I arrived at the house I opened the hall door and Paul and his two brothers were standing in the hallway. Not exactly the reunion I'd envisaged.

How bad do you think it is? Paul asked.

How bad is what? I asked jokingly.

The kitchen is going to need some silicone work to get rid of the rot, his older brother, Andrew answered.

That'll be expensive, Paul said.

But it has to be done, Denny said.

Yes, Paul sighed.

Look, Fuzz (Paul's childhood nickname), I'll hack the wall down in preparation. That'll save some of the cost, Andrew said.

It'll be such a mess, Paul said.

Tempers were always fraught when the three of them got together. My arrival allowed the two brothers off the hook. It also gave Paul an opportunity to dump on me.

You're looking very *sportif*, he bitched.

Thank you, I laughed.

It's all very well for *some* I suppose. Flying here, there and everywhere while the rest of us have to stay put, he quipped. I trust you *had* a good time? he asked. Contempt barely hidden in his voice.

As you can see we're all working very hard here, he added, getting in a dig at his brothers.

It was great, I replied ignoring his sarcasm. And I didn't break a leg.

Paul usually organised things for other people. In fact I often told him he did too much for people – when he'd let off steam about being too busy. He found it difficult to say no. He found it frustrating to be dependent on others, particularly his brothers. I fielded all his quips as the two brothers slunked off elsewhere. Soon the ice melted.

I told Paul about the nightmare I had in Italy.

You're overreacting, he said. Everything will be fine, he added.

I don't think I'll make this trip in May, I said.

I was due to go on a round-the-world trip the following May.

What do you think I should do? I asked.

You should go on the trip, he said.

You'll be in Cork until April, meanwhile I'll be making my recovery. When will you get another opportunity like this again? I'll join you in Florida in a couple of months. I can convalesce there for a month or two. We'll be together then, he said.

I wanted to believe that this would be happy-ever-after. I agreed. In many ways I was running away from the situation.

I was due to leave on the big trip early May. In the meantime I travelled up and down to Dublin at weekends. Paul was apparently making progress with his treatment and things seemed to be under control. I was looking forward to the trip, specially now that Paul would join me in Florida.

My head was full of plans – The Everglades and a trip to the Bahamas. I'd spent a holiday there a number of years before and thought it might be worth a second visit. Paul was a very experienced sailor and we planned to go scuba-diving. The whole affair held out the promise of paradise regained.

Chapter Three

My mother's mother died in February 1983. She always predicted that she'd die in February.

I was born, married and widowed in February, she told me when I was young. I know I'll die in February. I dread that month more and more each year I get older, she said.

Her death was my first experience of death at close quarters. The family gathered around her for the last few weeks of her life. She lay in a coma. I did the midnight to dawn vigil to allow other members of the family rest. I was impatient with the pace of things. The suspended animation of it all. Nobody doubted that she'd die soon. The question was when? I thought I could help matters along. I played with the idea of her death being an exchange for Paul's health. Frequently, during my stints at her bedside, I thought of smothering her with a pillow. She was 94. To swap her old life for his young life made perfect sense. But my anger about Paul's illness couldn't be salved by murdering my grandmother. I don't know whether it was its inherent illogicality or my cowardice that prevented me from acting out this fantasy. She eventually died, fighting for every last breath, because of her will to live. This happened amidst a chorus of some decade or other of the rosary. She had had a good innings. I was not saddened by her death. If anything, I was relieved. Now people could go back to their routines.

* * *

Paul read avidly. Medical journals and the like, to keep himself informed about his disease. We'd talked about AIDS as a possible cause of his illness. But little was known about AIDS at this time. Paul wasn't a drug-user. Nor had he been to America. So we ruled out the AIDS theory. We stuck to the doctor's diagnosis of cancer.

I spent a week in Dublin in late April just before the big trip. Paul and I had a late lunch in Fitzser's on Camden Street on the Saturday. We'd bought *two copies* of the paper to avoid any hassle as we browsed over lunch. This was a major climb-down on Paul's behalf – he was careful with money.

It's not within the budget, he'd say.

We did *The Irish Times* crossword together.

This is great, now I can do the crossword in peace, Paul said. Without you annoying me, he added slyly.

Sure, I quipped, looking at him. I was always able to finish the crossword before him.

I brought the AIDS theory up again that lunch-time. I'd read an article in a Canadian magazine *Body Politic* which described the disease and referred to its possible sexual transmission.

I'm worried about AIDS, Paul, I said. If you have it, Paul, then I could also have it.

The doctors would know if I had it, he said.

But what if you do have it? Paul. What if the doctors are wrong?

What do you mean if I have AIDS? he snapped.

Well, it's sexually transmitted, according to reports. That means that I could have it too, I replied.

Paul got angry and left abruptly. I sat there for a moment. I went to the till to pay for the food and followed him on to the street.

I'm just trying to sort this out, I explained to him outside the restaurant.

We're having a great weekend. I want to forget that I'm the one who's sick, why are you being so selfish? Paul shouted.

I'm not being selfish, I'm concerned for you and I'm worried for me also, I told him.

He stormed off.

I stood on the footpath wondering what to do. I saw him run across the road. I heard a screech of breaks and saw him fall to the ground.

Paul had run out in front of a car. He'd been knocked down. I ran to him.

Paul, are you all right? I asked.

Yes I'm fine. Help me up, he said reaching his hand out towards me.

He was only grazed and shaken. Thankfully. It could have been much worse. There were times in the months to come that I wished it *had* been worse.

We never discussed the AIDS theory again. Paul's response to his medication took a turn for the worse. It wasn't going as well as expected. He was distraught. Shook. He had considered alternative medicine but he opted for the conventional medicine route. The doctors decided that he should travel to London for further tests and more treatment. He was to go to the Marsden Hospital in London for treatment a few weeks after I left on my trip.

We spent some time plotting my itinerary, detailing all of the pit stops with hotel numbers and addresses during the last few days I was in Dublin. I wanted to be with Paul, but I also wanted to be let off this particular hook. Escape. The plan was that he'd call me every second week and we'd meet up in Florida in eight weeks – four phone calls later.

* * *

We spent my last day in Dublin sitting in the garden. We made love on the sitting-room sofa that afternoon, before I went back to Cork. The sun was blazing through the french window as the curtains wafted in the breeze. We lay together, silently, our arms and legs entwined. I could hear our heartbeats. I could also hear the carriage clock on the mantlepiece tick away the seconds as the time for my going drew closer. His illness stole nothing from our passion. But then sex had always played a big part in our relationship. It was the last time we made love in that complete, physical, way.

We looked at each other as I climbed into the taxi.

See you in Florida, Paul said.

Yes, I said. I smiled and swallowed the lump in my throat. Soon, in another place, everything would be better.

The train journey to Cork was abysmal. I began to cry in the taxi and was still crying when I arrived in Cork. I huddled into my train seat. I wasn't worried that I'd be tormented by a chatting nun, the usual blight of such trips. Who'd want to be with a blubbering mess like myself? A neighbour of my mother's was sitting nearby. She saw that I was crying. I was embarrassed and tried to control my tears. They stopped for a while but the sobbing went on. I had no control over tears or sobs. I couldn't explain why I was upset. I didn't understand it myself. I refused to see what was happening. I steeled myself and clung to the memory of our embraces, content in the smell of our sex, warm in its comfortableness. Yet, something, somewhere inside me knew that we'd never make love again.

People don't die like this – when you're in your twenties, I told myself. But I knew then that he was going to die. It was unbearable.

* * *

I walked along McCurtain Street after I got off the train. It was past midnight. And it was raining. I called to a pub that some friends ran. I sat in the bar while they cleared up and counted the takings. We had drinks and chatted. I told them that I didn't want to go on the trip and that Paul was going to die. They told me that I was feeling sorry for myself and overreacting. I let it go.

* * *

My college friend Mary married an older wealthy man. She became pregnant soon after they were married and gave birth to a baby boy. Her husband was anxious to have another child. But she wasn't in too much of a hurry. They planned a trip around the world before having a second child.

I stayed with them in Cork and helped them decorate their house. We got on well. I loved their baby and sometimes baby-sat for them.

How'd you like to go on a trip around the world? Mary asked me one morning when we were having breakfast.

I think I could handle it, at a push, I replied.

Do you think you could hack being my au-pair?

I love flouting convention, I replied.

We both laughed.

Seriously, Bren adores you and I'd hate to have a stranger around.

You've done a wonderful interview, Mr Philpott, she joked. The job's yours. We'll handle all the cost, and throw in a bit more. You'd work a day on and a day off. Your shift would start at six pm one day till six pm the next. And we'd alternate days with you. Occasionally we might go off for a few days at a time and you'd take care of the son and heir while we're gone, she explained.

Sounds good to me, I enthused.

I was buying time when I lived with Mary and her husband in Cork. I didn't know how long it would take for Paul and myself to work things out. It was limbo. I got on with life in Cork expecting to be back in Dublin before too long. Paul was convinced that I was in Cork for a no-good reason.

* * *

Our relationship changed. It started to change when I decided to go to Cork. The only option I had was to go back. I had taken all the abuse I was going to take. It still took a lot of courage to go.

I don't understand why you're still there, Paul said when he came to see me a few months after I moved back to Cork. Unless you're sleeping with her husband.

He couldn't, or wouldn't, understand why I was in Cork. And sleeping with Mary's husband would've been the last reason why I was there. But nothing could convince him otherwise.

I realise now that the power had shifted in our relationship. But Paul could only understand the change in terms of sex.

I remember a conversation I had with Donal Roche, who was then Paul's doctor.

Are you sleeping with anyone else? he asked me.

No. Why do you ask?

Paul believes you're sleeping with your friend's husband, he said. If that was the case, it would explain this type of fungal infection he has. It's normally associated with women and heterosexual sex. If you were sleeping with this married man, it would make sense. Otherwise. . .

But I'm not sleeping with anyone, I interrupted him.

Then this infection he has is a mystery, Donal replied. I believe what you're saying.

★ ★ ★

I watched a TV special on AIDS in a hotel in Brisbane. It was the usual run-of-the-mill type programme. It outlined the epidemiology of the disease. It spoke about the flurry the international scientific community was in in its attempt to find a cure for what they called the gay plague. I was fascinated – glued to the television.

I hated every moment of the trip. Here I was in the most amazing places and I didn't give a shit. The drive through the desert to the Grand Canyon was wonderful. I love deserts. I sat on an outcrop of rock over-looking the vast canyon. Breathtaking.

But I wanted to go home. To be with Paul.

I couldn't wait to get to Florida. To see him again.

I hadn't heard from Paul through the Far East,

Australia, Hawaii or California. I didn't call him either. I was afraid that he'd changed his mind and wouldn't travel to Florida. It didn't occur to me that he wouldn't be *able* to travel to Florida.

* * *

After eight weeks of playing happy tourist, around the Far East, Hawaii and the West Coast of America, I'd had enough. The next port of call was Cocoa Beach, a few miles from Florida's Cape Canaveral. It was Larry Hagman, aka Major Nelson of *I dream of Jeannie* land. We arrived there two weeks before some friends were due over from Ireland. They were to be married in Florida and we were to get the preparations under way. The fuss about the wedding didn't exactly fill me with enthusiasm.

I walked along the beach for miles each day. I'd take Bren, the baby with me on my days on. The beach in Florida was boring by Irish standards. It was flat and monotonous. But the sun compensated. Bren liked to play in the sand, and like all babies, delighted in the freedom of not wearing a nappy. One day he was sitting near me with his bucket and spade as he played with the sand. He wasn't wearing any clothes and I had covered his skin with a sun-block. I was reading a book.

Cover that child up, a woman's voice spoke aggressively.

What's the problem? I asked as I turned in her direction. I noticed passers-by look in our direction.

He's just a child, I replied.

It's not proper, she shouted.

Lady, the child's not doing anyone any harm, I said assertively.

Some pervert's probably looking at him right now from

those apartments, she said pointing to the buildings behind us. And will go out and rape somebody tonight. It'll be your fault.

I think you're overreacting, I said.

Bren was getting upset and began to cry. I picked him up and comforted him.

Will you take responsibility for this if it happens? The woman continued to shout as she walked away.

I ignored her and concentrated on calming Bren. Florida is full of weirdos, I thought.

It was also full of *wrinklies*. Old couples mainly. They'd spent too much time in the sun. The colour of their skin was just a few shades lighter than the large brassy gold jewellery they wore on their necks, wrists and ankles. I kept thinking about being separated from Paul as I walked past them. There was a bar a few miles down the beach from the apartment we lived in. It was a Vietnam veterans' hang out. These war survivors congregated in the sunshine state in large numbers. They could make ends meet better in Florida than elsewhere. They were strange people. I realised that Florida wasn't the place for me as I sat amongst these remnants of people, one day, drinking cold beer in the hot sun. They got drunk by day and shot at the stars by night. They scared me.

At this point my relationship with Mary's husband had deteriorated to mere civility. I was indifferent about our travels. And he believed that I was unappreciative. The fact was that I longed for Paul and wanted to be with him. So I cut the trip short. The decision felt like calamine lotion on sunburn. It was sheer relief. I had to be with Paul.

I announced my decision to go that evening after

dinner. The next morning Mary drove me to a local travel agent and I rearranged my flights. The travel agent booked me through, all the way to Cork.

The trip has been great, Mary, I said as we drove along the freeway. I really need to get back and see Paul.

But he hasn't called you during the trip, she said.

I know, I replied. But I have to see him. I can't get him out of my mind.

She dropped me off at a friend's who brought me to the airport later that afternoon. I felt relieved as the flight took off from Orlando Airport. And raindrops trickled against the plane's window.

Chapter Four

I'm sorry, sir, but we don't have any reservation for Philpott.

There must be some mistake, I said. My travel agent booked me through to Cork from Orlando.

When was this, sir?

This morning, I said as she tapped keys on the computer's keyboard.

Yes, we do have a booking for you to Cork from Heathrow, but there's nothing for you out of JFK.

Can you get me a seat on the flight anyway?

I'm sorry, sir, but the flight is full.

But I have to get out of New York tonight, I said, panicking.

The only seats available are in first class, sir.

I'll take one.

That will require a surcharge, sir.

Can I speak to a supervisor please?

Yes sir, can you stand aside while I call one. I moved to one side.

People were milling in the departure lobby. I looked around and wondered where I could spend the night if I couldn't get out of New York that evening.

Hello, she said smilingly. The supervisor was a beautiful tall black woman.

What can I do for you today, sir?

My booking to London isn't in the system. I flew in from Orlando this morning and was supposed to be booked through to Cork. I am in the system from London to Cork. But there's nothing showing for me out of JFK. I have to get home as quickly as possible. It's very urgent, I blabbered.

She looked at me and nodded reassuringly.

Let me check this out, I'll only be a moment, she said.

I watched her as she keyed information into a computer.

Obviously some gremlin has been at work in the system, she said. We can put you on this evening's flight. We've got some room in first class but it will require a surcharge.

I can't pay anything. I've got very little money, I said anxiously.

She scrutinised me for a moment. Then her face broke into a beautiful smile. That's no problem, Mr Philpott, she said. You're not responsible for this error. She punched some more information into the computer. Can I see your passport please? I handed it to her. She leafed through the green document.

Everything seems to be in order, she said, handing it back to me with my boarding pass tucked inside the front cover. Have an enjoyable flight and I apologise again for the mix up.

Thank you, I said smilingly.

* * *

JFK airport grew smaller as the plane climbed into the sky. Dusk fell as the lights of New York glistened in the distance below. The leg-room in the first class cabin was luxurious. I leaned into the spacious seat and wrapped myself in a blanket. I looked out on the twilight cloud banks and imagined Paul's anguished face in their different formations.

Would you care for an aperitif, sir? the hostess asked.

Yes. Some champagne please. And I won't be eating this evening, I said.

Enjoy your drink, sir, she said handing me the glass of champagne. Here's another one to keep you going, she said smiling as she handed me another snipe.

I drank quickly and then drifted off to sleep. When I woke up I realised I'd shattered a back tooth because I'd been grinding my teeth in my sleep.

* * *

I called a friend of Paul's, in Dublin, as soon as I got back to Cork.

Hello, it's Ger, I said.

Where are you? he asked.

I'm in Cork.

When did you get back?

This afternoon. I've been calling the house but I couldn't get through. Where's Paul?

There was a slight pause.

He's staying at the mews with his mother in Clonskeagh. He's been ill. When are you coming up?

First thing tomorrow, I said. Don't tell him I'm coming. I want it to be a surprise.

* * *

I arrived in Dublin the next day, July 4th, and went directly

46

to the mews. I saw Andrew through the glass door as I rang the doorbell.

Hello, he said. When did you get back?

Yesterday.

How was the trip? You obviously got good weather. You're sporting a fine tan, he said in his throaty voice.

Where's Paul? I asked.

Paul's resting upstairs, he said. Mother's gone out for the evening and I'm keeping an eye on Paul.

After what seemed like endless small talk, I climbed the spiral staircase and knocked on the bedroom door. I was full of excitement, anticipation and adrenalin. I was also nervous. Paul hadn't kept in touch with me during my trip and I'd thought that he mightn't want to see me. I opened the door of the small bedroom and saw a body huddled in the bed. My heart raced. Panic spread through my body. Nothing about him was like the Paul I knew, apart from his now very large glossy eyes. He had the characteristic big eyes of people with AIDS who are close to death. And they were the only thing that I recognised. He began to cry and I knelt at his bedside. I hugged and kissed him. The tears fell down my cheeks.

What had happened? His frame had disappeared. His weight was down to around seven stone. He was skin and bone. He had no hair. Anywhere. I felt that I'd gone crazy. This couldn't be happening. Why the fuck hadn't his brother told me? How could he let me walk into this unprepared? I acted, or thought I did, as if nothing unusual had happened. My heart was breaking. I was in pain but I felt I had to stay in control.

We clung on to each other. Comforting each other. When the embrace broke I'd have to react. What was I going to do? What was going on?

What are you going to do now? Are you home for good? Will you stay in Dublin? Paul's hesitant questions broke the silence.

I'm staying here to get you better, I said confidently. And then we'll get on with the rest of our lives. I'm never leaving you again.

When I got your postcard from San Francisco I thought that you'd fallen in love with someone and wouldn't come back, he said.

I'd sent him a postcard from San Francisco saying *I left my heart in San Francisco* . . . I hate writing postcards and the card from San Francisco was meant as a joke.

I've missed you so much. I thought you weren't coming back, he said. I'm sorry for all the problems last year, he added.

Forget about it, I said cutting him off. Now was not the time to go into his infidelities!

The treatment in the Marsden Hospital didn't work, he said. It tipped me over the edge. Apparently, my system was weakened by the chemo I got here. And the dosage they gave me in England was too strong and wiped me out.

What sort of prognosis are we talking? I asked. I couldn't believe that such an enormous change could happen so quickly.

They're not sure. It's a question of waiting to see how the body will react, he said.

It was obvious that his days were numbered. But I was scared to talk about it. It was easier to pretend that he'd get better. I managed a smile and stroked his arm. He lit a cigarette and coughed when he inhaled. His beautiful blue eyes were dancing in his head, watching me.

* * *

Paul brightened up considerably after I came back. He'd lost interest in eating. But I cajoled him to eat again for a while.

Paul has perked up a lot since you've arrived, his mother said to me a few days after I returned. He's even eating again. Whatever you're doing, it's working. Keep it up.

I'm a good cook and Paul liked my creme caramel. He asked for it every day for about a week. He'd lie on the sofa watching me as I put the elaborate dessert together. The ritual with the custard, burning the sugar and the setting up of the home-made bain marie was a welcome distraction from Paul's illness. I consoled myself that he was getting wholesome nourishment. But I was getting more out of the comfort food than he was. His weight didn't come back and Paul soon tired of the favoured dessert. But his spirits did, however, remain up.

I did some odd painting jobs for his mother so I could be near him each day. I'd pick up his Major cigarettes and *The Irish Times* each morning on my way from Ranelagh to Clonskeagh.

* * *

Do you still want to be a teacher? he asked one sunny day when we were sitting on the sheltered patio.

Yes, I do.

I've been thinking a lot lately about the derelict farm near the cottage, Paul said.

And? I asked.

I thought that when I'd get better I'd sell Mount Pleasant Avenue. Buy the farm and restore it.

I don't know if I want to live in Wicklow all the time, I said.

I've thought of that, he said. We could buy a flat together in town. That way we'd have the best of both worlds. What do you think?

I think it's a great idea. We could buy a floor in one of those houses on Elgin Road. And I could get a teaching job in town. *You've* certainly brightened up over the past few days, I said.

He'd been despondent. And now at last there was a plan. There was to be light at the end of the tunnel. Paul had spoken about the farm for a couple of years before his illness. The idea of becoming a teacher came to me the previous winter.

* * *

These days were strangely idyllic. Our relationship had been turbulent in the past.

If Denny and my father didn't believe in monogamy, why should I? Paul would argue.

Because I'm not going out with your father or your brother. If you want a relationship with me there isn't room for other people, I'd reply.

Paul had sex with whomever he wanted, whenever he wanted. And I found out. *He was a bastard*.

Now he wasn't unfaithful anymore. The tension about that was gone. But I didn't want to pay such a high price for this new-found tranquillity. I wanted a healthy Paul. Not an invalid. That wasn't on the cards.

* * *

I'd sit with Paul in his room most evenings and walk the half-hour back to Ranelagh in the early hours of the morning. Paul had a nasty cough that got worse late at night. His smoking didn't help. And he couldn't be persuaded to give them up. So the cough kept him awake. A friend of Paul's was given marijuana as part of his treatment for testicular cancer when he was in America. Paul thought dope might help him to relax and help his appetite loss. I was given some money and I bought some hash for him.

Do you remember the first time we bought dope? I asked him as he lay in bed and I rolled a joint.

Yes I do, he said. Now where was it?

No, you don't remember, I said looking at him.

He smiled.

It was in that pub in Dorset Street, he countered. And I remember Noel gave out to me for being irresponsible and said you were a bad influence.

No, it wasn't in Dorset Street. That was another time. It was in the Jetfoil on the quays, I said.

That's right, he laughed. And so much for you being cool. You were terrified.

Dead right I was scared, I said. I'd to wait outside in the car while you went in to score the dope. Ready to drive off as soon as you emerged with the stash, I said. Someone told you to walk to a hatch at the back of the pub, knock and hand in your money in return for which you'd get a tinfoil-wrapped piece of dope. I remember I was terrified that the Drug Squad would raid the place while you were inside.

That night seemed far away now, I thought. It was fun to sit with Paul and smoke joints. It helped him sleep. And it helped me to forget.

* * *

The days ran slowly into each other. Slow was also the best word to describe Paul at this time. Some days it took him until five in the afternoon to get out of bed, have a bath and get dressed. His mobility wasn't great and he was irritable. He hated being helped, even getting in and out of the bath. I'd sit on the loo chatting to him while he soaked in the warm water. But sometimes he wanted to be alone. The water helped to take pressure from his bony body. After bathing he'd climb carefully, one step at a time, down the spiral staircase. And then would install himself on the sofa and listen to the radio or read. I'd read aloud to him. We'd do *The Irish Times* crossword together. Often, it took forever to finish. But that I could deal with.

Paul was incontinent at times and that bothered him. Sometimes, he wouldn't make it to the bathroom in time. Other times he'd do it while he was in the bath. Horrible to see the shame on his face when that happened or when he accidentally soiled the floor. Cleaning up his spills was awful. Not because I was mopping up pools of diarrhoea. But because the incontinence marked his decline. It marked the disintegration of the man I loved. And now I was taking care of him. He was as helpless as a baby. But I didn't fall in love with a baby. His illness, his emaciation was one thing. To see him struggle to try and cope with the loss of his bodily functions was something entirely different.

I felt that the goalposts of our relationship had been moved. I didn't choose to be in this situation. But I didn't have any other option. I still loved him but in a way that I could never have imagined. It was pitiful to see him fight to hold on to his dignity. There was nothing that I could do to stop what was happening.

* * *

Paul called his solicitor to come and draw up his will the day he was due to go into the hospital for some tests. The solicitor asked me to witness the will. I knew from my law studies that this meant that I wouldn't inherit anything from Paul. This peeved me a little. I also found it amusing.

* * *

You really get upset about this inheritance stuff, I'd said to Paul, about two years earlier, after a row about how he felt his brother, Denny took advantage of things.

He doesn't work hard and expects things to fall into his lap. Life isn't like that, Paul said of Denny. And he stormed out of the house.

I never want this kind of hassle with money and inheritances, I said later that evening when tempers had cooled down.

So you don't want anything if something should happen to me? he asked.

No, I said.

Are you sure?

Absolutely, I replied.

I thought of this conversation as I signed the witness declaration on the will. And would remember it again in the not-too-distant future.

* * *

Paul had a short stay in hospital for some tests. They'd performed so many fucking tests on him and nobody was any wiser about what was going on. I didn't have much money at the time. So I'd walk to the hospital and take the bus part of the way home. I'd work out different scenarios in my head as I walked to the hospital. Then and later, when he was re-hospitalised, I'd visit him in the late afternoons and stay with him till late into the night.

I'd walk through Donnybrook, along the dual carriageway, past RTE and down towards the Merrion Road. I felt sorry for myself and angry that none of the people driving by knew what was going on. I'd pass between the hospital morgue and the private hospital as I made my way to the public section of St Vincent's hospital. I grew to hate that hospital. The ritual of walking through the busy hallway. Taking the lift to Paul's floor and making my way down the corridor to his room. Often there'd be other visitors there, who'd usually left when I arrived. I was glad to be alone with Paul.

One day when I arrived in Paul's room I burst into tears. I couldn't help it.

What's wrong? You mustn't cry, Paul said.

I want you to come home, I explained.

I'll come home soon. But I can't deal with you being upset like this. I don't like to see you cry. Promise me you won't cry anymore. Your smile helps me get better, Paul told me.

I promised myself that I'd never cry in front of him again. But I couldn't manage to keep the tears in once I was outside the hospital. Usually I cried at the bus shelter outside the hospital and in the bus as it travelled along Merrion Road. People must have thought I was a loony. Nobody ever asked me why I was crying. I'd have loved it if someone had asked. But, I don't know if I could've dealt with such a question. I got off at the stop opposite Jury's Hotel in Ballsbridge. By the time I reached Mount Pleasant Avenue, my tears would have stopped, after the walk along the canal. I hated going into the empty house and sleeping in Lord Londonderry's second best bed.

* * *

My life at this time was split in two. I was active in the abortion amendment campaign and met lots of new people. There was a great feeling of camaraderie. I didn't tell people about Paul being ill. I needed to have something for myself. And anyway what would I have said?

Some old college friends would come to Mount Pleasant avenue for dinner. I'd cook elaborate meals.

Your middle name is *Food*, they joked.

I imagined Paul was there. I'd give him a blow-by-blow account of who the dinner guests were, what I cooked, and a running commentary on the conversation. I would have liked my friends to have visited Paul in hospital. But it would have been unfair to ask them, and I felt Paul might have felt embarrassed. So I didn't broach the subject.

* * *

I always feel like the odd one out with that crowd, I told a friend as we pushed our bikes past the Gardens of Remembrance on our way to the Grapevine Arts Centre garden party one Saturday afternoon.

What do you mean? he asked.

Well, they're all image, with attitude to burn.

I know what you mean, he said. And we both laughed.

The garden was a bit dilapidated. The food was shite. But the music, as always, was great. And the drugs plentiful.

Come inside, my pal called from one of the windows at the back of the building. I went inside and found him with a scissors and a spray tin of blue hair colour.

New image coming up, sir, he giggled. Here light this joint as I turn you into a new you, he said.

He slashed at my T-shirt with the scissors and sprayed my hair blue.

What do you think? he asked as I looked at my make-over in the cracked mirror.

Somehow, I don't think this is quite me, I said.

You're never happy, he said dragging me out into the garden where everyone was dancing.

That was a great party, I thought as I cycled home. The clock on the Harp Building struck ten as I cycled over O'Connell bridge. It was a balmy evening. And my mood was up for the first time in ages. I heard noises from the front bedroom window as I wheeled the bike through the gate of number nine Mount Pleasant Avenue. It sounded as if someone was moving furniture. It must be Paul's brothers, I thought as I rushed up the stairs to the bathroom for a piss. Odd. The bathroom window was open. But I'd locked all the windows before going out this afternoon? I heard noises from my bedroom as I came out of the bathroom. I looked up towards the door on the top landing and saw two men come out of my bedroom. I can't remember anything about them except that one was younger than the other.

What . . . Shit! I shouted and jumped down the stairs into the hallway and ran out the front door. I climbed over the railings into the next-door neighbours' garden and rang their doorbell.

Somebody's broken into the house and they're still inside. Call the guards, I said.

Go out to the garden the neighbour said to his two sons, and I'll go in through the house with you, he said to me.

I followed him into the hallway and out into the garden. We saw the men jump off the garage into a laneway that ran behind the houses. We went back into the kitchen and I made tea.

Do you want me to stay? the neighbour asked when the police arrived.

No. I'll be okay, I answered.

There were three plainclothes policemen.

What's your name? one of them asked. And tell us exactly what happened?

They looked strangely at me. At first I couldn't make out why. But then I remembered my blue hair and cut-up T-shirt.

I was at a party this evening and when I came back I heard noises from my bedroom when I came up the path. I thought that it must have been Paul's brothers. They have keys to the house. I ran upstairs to go to the toilet and noticed that the bathroom window was open. I thought this was strange because I'd closed all the windows before I went out. When I came out of the bathroom I saw two men come out of my bedroom. I ran out and called the neighbours.

Where did the men go?

I presume they went out through the bathroom window.

Who's Paul?

Paul is my friend. He's ill and in hospital. I'm staying in the house on my own.

Were you drinking this evening?

Yes I was.

Are you drunk?

Not now. But I was earlier. Why are you asking me these questions? Shouldn't you be taking fingerprints or something?

We're organising that. Can you call someone to stay in the house with you tonight?

All Paul's family are away for the weekend. Why? Do you think they'll be back? I asked.

No, it's just a precaution, one of them answered.

I rang a college friend who was working in Dublin and he and his girlfriend came to spend the night with me.

Has anything been stolen?

I don't know.

We'll drop by tomorrow and check with you, they said as they left.

★ ★ ★

I went to a rally for the anti-amendment campaign in St Stephen's Green the next day. My friend Kay had organised it. It was a big success. But I felt like a zombie. The break-in had set me off balance. I went home before nightfall. I wanted to be inside the house before it got dark. When I got back to the house I searched every room. Behind doors and curtains, under the beds, in wardrobes. Anywhere that someone could hide. I closed all the curtains and checked that all the doors and windows were locked. Then I went to bed.

The following night someone tried to break into the

house again. I heard them on the roof of the return. I called the guards.

It's probably the same people, one guard told me.

It's normal for thieves to try a second time, the second guard explained.

I got a two-year-old collie-type dog on loan from the animal shelter. I figured that he'd be familiar with the name boy. So I called him boy. He was a good watchdog and company for me.

Chapter Five

Paul's spirits began to flag. He became listless and withdrawn. Before this happened we had walked daily up and down the corridor of the hospital. He preferred to walk backwards and forwards on his corridor than anywhere else in the hospital. I loved the to-ing and fro-ing. It broke the monotony and terror of watching him in bed all the time. And I believed that the exercise would build up his strength and help him back to full health.

I don't want to walk in the corridor anymore, Paul said one evening.

Why? The exercise is good for you. It will help you get strong, I said.

I hate people looking at me. Shuffling along. I wouldn't be able to stand without leaning on you, he said. I looked at him and knew that what he said was true. Who could blame him? It wasn't exactly the most riveting jaunt imaginable. I was terrified. But I said nothing.

Paul was in an isolation room. It had a small vestibule. There was a sink to wash hands in and some gowns which nobody ever wore. It had a glass viewing window. I lay on the bed next to Paul with his head resting on my arm. I held his right hand to my mouth. His thumb in my mouth. An IV-drip attached to his left arm.

He's lying on the bed with him and he's sucking his thumb, she said.

60

I heard a woman's voice say these words. And then some giggling. I opened my eyes. It was dark. We'd drifted off to sleep. We must have slept for two hours. I turned towards the viewing window and saw two nurses outside. I felt embarrassed at first. And then angry that they'd disturbed our solitude. I turned away as they left. Paul was still sleeping. It felt good to have him sleep in my arms. I felt safe protecting him. Yet I knew it was over. That it was coming to an end. I was scared. But I shut these thoughts out of my mind.

I gently prised my arm from under his head and climbed off the bed. He was still sleeping. Good, I haven't disturbed him, I thought. I went to the bathroom and splashed water on my face.

You'd better get yourself a big cushion, a friend had said, that September, when I'd gone to Cork to vote in the abortion referendum. I remembered her words as I looked in the mirror in his bathroom. I was at sea. Lost in a morass of confusion.

I kissed his cheek before leaving the room. He was still asleep. At least he's getting some rest tonight, I thought as I made my way out into the cold night air.

* * *

Denny and I planned a surprise for Paul. We decided to organise a helicopter trip to lift his flagging spirits.

We were very enthusiastic about our plans when we spoke to Paul about it.

It will be too expensive, Paul said

Don't worry about that, Denny answered.

Where would we go? Paul asked.

Wherever you'd like to go, I replied.

I'd like to go to the cottage, he said. And out to sea. He was sitting with his head bent like an old man.

We'll throw in a trip over the city to cover all the options, I added jokingly.

And Paul smiled. It was the first time in a while that he smiled.

But here was a slight problem. Paul didn't want to leave his room since he'd stopped his daily walks. How would we get him out of the hospital and into a helicopter? Paul, you must start walking again. It's good for you.

I don't like the way people stare at me, Paul said.

I'll be with you, I said. Let them stare. It'll be fun. He nodded unconvincingly.

Nontheless one sunny day, about a week later, I persuaded him that we should go outside and stroll around the hospital grounds.

It's a beautiful day, Paul. Let's go outside, I said.

I'm too weak, he replied.

The sun will be good for you. And we can use one of the wheelchairs, I persisted.

Okay. But only for a short while, he agreed.

He put on his dressing-gown while I went into the corridor to get the wheelchair. I pushed the wheelchair next to the bed. I helped Paul hang his legs down the side of the bed and held his arm while he swung into the wheelchair. Paul put on an old knitted cap. And I wrapped him snugly in a Foxford rug. We set off.

Hello Denny. How are you? I said as we met him in the corridor on our way to the lift. I was very up.

Are you coming with us? Paul asked from his slumped position in the wheelchair. We're going outside for a stroll.

Yes, if that's all right? Denny replied looking at me. I nodded. And the three of us set off together.

The journey in the lift, through the hospital foyer and outside, was effortless. Paul was a little upset when people stared at him but seemed to enjoy himself all the same. We walked around the grounds. Denny and I took turns pushing Paul's wheelchair. We stopped and chatted.

This is my first time outdoors for over a month, Paul said.

Why don't you stand up and take a few steps? I encouraged.

I don't feel strong enough, he answered anxiously.

It's okay. Just a few steps. You can do it, I continued. He looked at me and made a small nodding gesture. This is working, I thought as I watched him prepare to get out of the wheelchair. If only Paul could take a few steps, everything would be better. He began to lift himself out of the chair. When he was almost upright he flopped back into the chair and began to cry.

I want to go inside. Please don't make me stay outside anymore. I hate being out here. It reminds me of how sick I am. I want to go back to my room, he pleaded.

I was shocked. I felt like a bully. Paul had come outside with us, not because he wanted to, but because we gave him no choice. Denny and I were desperate that he shouldn't die. Denny didn't want a dead brother. And I didn't want a dead partner. It was crystal clear, however, that we'd pushed what we wanted too far. There'd be no helicopter trip.

I'll head off now, Denny said. Running away from emotions again I thought as I looked at him.

Thank you, Paul said when we were back in the room. I don't want to be bothersome.

No bother, Paul. I'm sorry for forcing you outside, I said. We hugged and he cried.

* * *

When Paul was obviously close to death his older brother decided that his house should be rented to somebody up-market.

It would be a more desirable property if an up-market so-and-so lived there, he said when he explained his plan to me. I was dumbstruck. This news would be crushing for Paul. It also meant that I'd have nowhere to live. That I was to be thrown out.

When is all this happening? I asked. I could arrange for some friends to move in and pay rent, I added.

The tenant, an up-market antique-dealer, will move in on the first of October, he replied. The house will get a better price when it's sold, he continued. I realised that this was already planned and not just an idea. The feelings of a dying man didn't enter into the equation. The plans were put in train and the deal signed without Paul's consent.

* * *

Have you heard about the plans for number nine? asked an older gay friend of Paul's, also from Cork, when I met him on the street a few days later.

You mean has my eviction notice been served? I joked dryly. He looked closely at me.

This will kill Paul when he finds out, said the man who was a family friend. That brother of his is an awful bollocks, he said in his Cork accent.

* * *

I made plans to move in with some friends in Santry. Luckily I found a flat in town. And I was spared the ordeal of living in northside suburbia. I learned that Paul was told about the arrangements for the house on Thursday September 29th.

He was distraught when I visited him that evening. We were alone in the hospital room. He lay crying. Huddled foetal-like, his back to the door, his head turned toward the window.

What's wrong? I asked stroking his hand.

They've given up hope, he blubbered.

Who has given up hope? I asked.

The family have. My mother and brothers, he said. They've taken my house away. They never consulted me about it. It's not fair. They should have asked my opinion, he said.

I sat on the bed consoling him. I held his head against my chest. Paul couldn't bear to have the covers over him. It hurt too much. Though his body had shrunk, his genitals had not. His older brother decided not to visit Paul in hospital because he found looking at him too upsetting. His skeletal hairless and nude body disturbed him.

I don't think I'm going to go to the hospital to see Fuzz anymore, he told his mother one day. I find the whole thing too upsetting. And frankly it's all rather embarrassing to have him lying there naked in front of the wife.

He didn't, however, care about upsetting Paul with the arrangements he had made for Paul's house.

I could kill his brother, I thought as we sat silently on the bed, Paul's sobs punctuating the silence. I stared at the wall, feeling the pins-and-needles run through my arm. I needed to change position to stop it from going dead but I didn't want to disturb Paul. It was good to hold him. But I didn't know what to do. Why is this happening? The question screamed in my head.

What will you do? asked Paul breaking the silence. Where will you live?

I've found a flat off Pembroke Street, I explained. We talked about the flat. The colour I'd paint the walls and the floor. What sort of furniture I'd get. Paul began to cry again.

It's no use, he said. I can't go on. I need everyone's support. Now they've given up on me, there's only you. You won't be strong enough to pull me through this.

I didn't know what to say. I sat holding his hand late into the night as darkness filled the room.

* * *

I saw Paul alive last – if you can call it alive – the following morning. I arrived at the hospital with his younger brother to find his mother with him. He was extremely distressed and, though sedated, he was not unconscious. He was incoherent: struggling to say something. He didn't make any sense. He looked miserable and unhappy as his eyes moved from one of us to the other. It felt like the magic boomerang had been thrown but hadn't quite made a proper flight. I could hear the others talk in what seemed a light-hearted way about something or other. I remember hearing laughter as I watched Paul try to speak. It was as if his brain wasn't in gear, his tongue was out of control. He couldn't make an intelligible sound. He was lost in a sea of bed linen, his head just visible propped against the pillow. We looked into each other's eyes. His large and shiny, bathed in tears, were scared. I hoped mine didn't give away my terror.

He'll be okay, his mother said when I was leaving.

I'll come and see you this evening, Paul, I told him, not sure that he could hear me.

His gaze followed me as I walked through the door. I waved to him through the viewing window. I didn't visit him that evening. I came down with a cold. I rang in and said I'd come the next day. He died early the next morning before I got to the hospital. He died alone. No one there to hold his hand. To give him permission to go. My nightmare while skiing in Italy had come to pass. Paul died, distressed and abandoned, in a hospital. The news about the house didn't kill him. But it didn't help him either. Through his last few miserable days.

★ ★ ★

I was staying in Denny's, his brother's, flat for a week or so. The phone rang early on the Saturday morning.

Hello? I said.

Ger, is Denny there? Paul's mother asked in her matter-of-fact way.

No, he's in Killeagh doing some work for Sean, I answered. He said he'd call me around ten this morning to check on Paul, I added. There was a momentary silence. Is anything wrong?

Ger, Paul's passed on. He's dead, she said.

When did this happen? I asked mesmerised by the finality of it. *He was dead*.

I got a call from the hospital this morning. They said

he wasn't feeling too well and that I'd better come in. I got organised and before I'd left they called back to say that he'd expired, she said. I was thrown by her clinical language. But she was the master of the stiff upper lip. And always concealed her emotions.

Why hadn't she called me earlier, I wondered. I looked at the clock. It was 9.15am.

His body is in the hospital . . . she said.

I don't want to see it.

Will you tell Denny when he calls? she asked.

Yes, I replied.

I put the receiver down. And picked it up immediately. I dialled the number.

Hello, my sister Joan answered her phone.

Joan, he's dead. Paul died this morning, I said.

Where are you? she asked. I'll come and get you.

No. I need to be by myself.

Are you certain?

Yes.

Is there anyone with you?

No.

Ger, are you in Denny's flat?

Yes.

I can be there in *half-an-hour*, she said.

No. Honestly, I'd prefer to be on my own. I'll talk to you later, I said and hung up.

I put the kettle on. There was a record on the turntable. I played it and made some coffee. I sat at the picture window of the top floor flat drinking coffee. I looked at the Dublin mountains. I can't describe how I felt. Slowly, I began to cry. I couldn't believe he wouldn't draw breath again. How would I carry on? *Everyone needs a holiday from their neighbourhood* . . . Marc Almond crooned from the stereo. Shit! What kind of music were they playing? I thought as I called my friend Patsy.

Philpott, I don't know what to say, she said when I told her Paul had died. Are you all right? Do you want me to come in?

No, I need to be on my own, I said. I replayed the record over and over again. The phone rang.

Hello, I said picking it up.

Good morning, Ger, Denny said.

Denny, Paul's dead.

When?

Your mother called over half-an-hour ago. He died early this morning.

I knew I shouldn't have gone away, he said. I'll come back right away, he added.

Drive carefully, Denny.

Bye.

Bye.

My vision blurred as I lay my head on the dark green tablecloth. I didn't know what to do.

★ ★ ★

I'd arranged to meet my parents and some childhood friends at a Masters swimming competition that afternoon. I walked to the Ringsend pool, near Denny's flat, several times that morning. It didn't sink in that 1.30 was 1.30 and no matter how often I walked to the pool, they wouldn't be there until 1.30. Walking along the road, struggling with my tears, felt better, than being inside the flat. Time was moving slowly. The sun was shining and the warmth felt good. Paul would never feel this sensation again. I was very angry but I knew that I was safer outdoors.

When I was back at the flat I felt like smashing everything. I walked to Paul's mother's house and got there by noon. Paul's older brother was with her and they were destroying Paul's papers – the treasure trove from the lacquered cabinet. I fought desperately to keep from crying. Stiff upper lip was the order of the day. Paul's solicitor arrived and I remember his mother asking about the details of his will.

Is there anyone outside the family involved? she asked. The solicitor looked in my direction. I turned away.

No, he said.

That's good, it makes things much simpler, she said.

I'd never felt so alone. I hadn't a fucking clue what was going on. I walked to the pool again. This time my folks and friends were there. As I walked towards the spectator's gallery, I knew from my parents' expressions that they'd heard of Paul's death. I wanted them to make things better. To feel safe in their embrace. I kissed my mother and my father shook my hands, holding the grip longer than usual.

Joan told us that Paul died this morning. We're very sorry. Are you okay? they asked.

I don't remember which one of them said what. They were the first people I'd met since Paul died who I felt were on my side. But I didn't want to have this conversation. I'd no control over anything. I could see lots of familiar faces. People that I'd spent countless hours with in swimming-pools. It felt safe. Proper that I was here now. I wanted to suspend thought.

Later my mother and I went to the bar for coffee.

I don't know what's going on, or what to do, I told her.

It's just one of those things, you'll get over it, she said.

It wasn't *just one of those things*, I told her. If one of

my brothers' girlfriends had died you wouldn't say that, I snapped.

We sat looking at each other without talking. My father joined us. It was very reassuring to be with them. Through the silence I could feel their love. I knew this wasn't easy for them either.

Come with us this evening, they said.

I nodded and we headed for my sister's house in Swords. When we arrived there her two sons, aged eleven and seven, were in the driveway.

We're sorry that Paul is dead, said Graham the elder of the two.

Yes I am too, said Russell the younger one.

I broke down and went inside to cry on my sister's shoulder.

Get it all out. It's no good bottling it up inside, she said.

Would you like to go for a pint? my father asked later that evening.

No, I'm going to go to bed, I answered.

* * *

I went back to Denny's flat the next afternoon.

Are you okay? my parents asked when they dropped me off.

Yes, I said as I nodded. I didn't look back at their car as they pulled away from the kerb. I felt like running after the car. But I couldn't.

* * *

When Paul was ill I promised myself that, if he got better,

I'd be prepared not to see him again. I just wanted him to live, I said to a friend as we ate dinner. It was a Sunday evening. The night before his funeral. There were five of us. The host and his partner, Denny and Colm, his partner. Two couples and myself. Paul had always been there when I'd eaten in this company before. I was fighting hard to keep my act together.

How selfless and mature that was of you, our host commented.

It wasn't really, I said. I was trying to make a pact with a higher power. I could imagine life without Paul, if only he were alive. But he'd figure out some way of being with me. Leaving my pact intact, I added. I hadn't at all *imagined* life without Paul. Paul dead.

Will you drive me to the flower market in the morning? I asked the host's partner.

Yes, he replied. I'll ring your bell at seven am.

I dragged on some clothes when the doorbell rang early the next morning. This is unbelievable, I thought. I watched my reflection in Denny's Art Deco mirror as I brushed my teeth.

How will I get through this day? I asked myself.

We drove in silence through the waking city to the flower market. I couldn't bear the thought of buying a pre-packaged wreath for Paul's grave. That would be such a bizarre thing to do, I thought. What flowers will I buy? I asked myself as we made our way towards the flower banks in the market. They stood out from the rest of the masses of colour. Deep blue bunches of statis. I bought several of them. They chose themselves. I never imagined that I'd have to buy flowers for my partner's grave.

When we got back to Denny's flat the others were eating breakfast. There was a queue for the bathroom as people got ready for the funeral.

Ger, can you arrange for a lift to the church for yourself? Denny asked me as people were leaving for the church – University chapel on St. Stephen's Green.

How are *you* getting there? I asked.

With the family, he replied looking at the ground. We'd been through this together, we'd helped each other. And now I was being jettisoned.

No problem, I answered. This is weird, I thought. They don't want me to go to the church with them. I wasn't to be a part of the family group in the church.

I'll give you a lift, Ger.

Eric, a friend who'd returned from England for the funeral, overheard Denny. I got dressed. I wore the grey suit my parents had bought for my graduation the previous summer. I cut off my little ponytail and put it in my pocket.

* * *

When we arrived at the church I went inside. I didn't know what to do. I saw the coffin at the top left hand side of the church and thought about going up to it. I decided not to. I could see Paul's family, some relatives and friends, sitting together near the coffin. I felt that I didn't have permission to sit in front with his family. I sat in the middle of the church and the service began. I heard footsteps walking up the aisle. I looked to my left and saw her. It was Susan Denham. She was a family friend. She sat next to the family in their pew. She wore black. Paul hadn't seen her for a number of years. How come *she's* sitting with them? I thought.

My mind wandered back to the sermon being

delivered by the priest from Glenstal Abbey – Paul's old school. He talked about Paul's life. What he was saying had to do with Paul's past. He didn't talk about his sexuality. He didn't talk about his relationship with me. And the more it went on, the less it had to do with Paul and the more it had to do with the family. The ritual. What he said didn't allow me to grieve. It made me feel as if it was all a mistake, a bad dream, it hadn't really happened. Because it didn't resonate with Paul's life – with our life.

A soprano sung Abide with Me. I broke down then. I felt I shouldn't be there. I dug my chin into my chest. My nose was snotty. And I didn't have a hanky. I was a mess. I was hot. I felt smothered, as if I was buried alive. This cannot be happening, I thought. I was confused. Everything I heard, everything going on around me, told me that I shouldn't be there. My chin was hurting my chest. I fixed on that sensation. I felt abandoned. Abused. Alone.

I wanted to scream.

Hold your dignity, I remembered my mother telling us when we were growing up. But my partner was dead. I'd never feel his embrace again. The warmth of his breath on my neck. These were the thoughts that ran through my head as I battled against the drone of the priest's sermon.

I'll never see him again, I said to myself.

Paul's mother and elder brother hurried out of the Church. I couldn't decide whether it was more like a wedding or the Olympic Games. I waited for a polite period. Others passed by. Then I walked down the aisle. My head still buried in my chest.

I felt watched and ignored. At the same time. My presence was an embarrassment. The journey seemed endless. Every step an enormous effort. I didn't know what I was going to do when I got outside. Suddenly, my arms were seized. Joan, my sister and Patsy, my friend, supported me.

Philpott, hang in there, Patsy urged.

Ger, keep it together, Joan encouraged.

I leaned into their support. *Blessed art thou* . . .

★ ★ ★

Paul's mother and brother were at the door of the church; receiving condolences. I didn't want to pass them. But I couldn't be inside the church a moment longer. I walked out of the darkened building towards the daylight and offered them my condolences. Like any Joe Soap on the street.

Then I ran across the road. I dodged between cars, not caring if I was knocked down. I needed the sanctuary of Stephen's Green. It was easy to cry in the church because, for all intents and purposes, I wasn't there. Outside the church, however, it was different. I needed privacy to cry.

Chapter Six

You must keep it together! I repeated my sister's words to myself as Eric and I drove through Fairview and headed for the coast road to Howth. I didn't want to go to the graveyard. But that wasn't my problem. My problem was I didn't know where else to go. And would I lose it and create a scene when I got there? The church service was one of *the* greatest indignities I'd ever experienced. To go to the cemetery was adding insult to injury. But it was Paul's funeral.

The sea glistened in the sunlight. I strained my eyes to make out the graveyard in the distance. How did it come to this? The lights at Sutton Cross took for ever to turn green. I told myself that I must get through the ordeal. We pulled in near St Fintan's cemetery. I sat and watched people haemorrhage from their cars. I felt degraded. And the sun shone brilliantly in counterpoint.

Cars lined the road in both directions for as far as I could see. I wanted to puke. But I tensed my stomach muscles hard as I did when I was a kid and didn't want to vomit in the car. And be jeered at by my brothers. Sea-dogs capped the rolling waves on the bit of sea glimpsed through the hawthorn trees.

Take care of yourself, Ger, he said as he grasped my arm.

He was an older, gay, man. He wore a red scarf. His

name was Pat. I looked into his eyes. I smiled. Thankful for his kindness. And nodded.

It's fucking awful, he said shaking his head as he walked away.

I made my way to the upper field where Paul was to be buried. That's where the crowd was gathering. An old ditch divided the two fields. People were backed up on the narrow path surrounding the grassed, graved area. His family stood by Paul's coffin over towards the lower end of the field. Fresh earth was mounded in a heap. It was difficult to stand as people surged into the upper field. I stepped on to the grass to avoid falling. I wanted to stand next to the coffin. To touch it. To take my rightful place. But I couldn't.

I realised that I was standing in the middle of the grass. Apart from the crowd. Away from the family. People all around. I spread my legs to steady myself, a trick I'd learned from my father during the Corpus Christi procession. I fingered the lock of my hair in the pocket of my charcoal grey wool graduation suit. I'll throw this in the grave later, I thought.

I was joined by two others.

Are you okay? one asked.

It's a beautiful fucking day isn't it? I thought.

It was a friend and Denny's boyfriend, Colm.

I knew that we were being watched. They're the faggots, is what I thought the watchers were thinking . . . And we were. The three of us stood in the middle. With many other gay men scattered throughout the crowd.

I walked against the traffic of people as they left the graveyard. I stood over the grave and looked into it. I kissed the lock of hair and dropped it on top of the coffin. Embarrassed. I couldn't make sense of any of this.

* * *

Will you join us for a drink? We're going to go to our cousin Jennifer's house, asked Paul's older brother.

Everyone else was going, including my lift, I thought. Yes, I replied. What happens next? I asked myself.

I climbed into Eric's car and we climbed the Hill of Howth. We turned off the main road and drove down a hill. The gateway was on the left-hand side. The driveway curved down to a lawn in front of the house. It was a large lived-in house. People were gathered in a drawing-room and drinks were served. I saw him in the distance. He was holding court in the centre of a group. They chatted and laughed as if they were at a cocktail party. He was Paul's first love. A schoolboy crush. I resented that he was there. I walked towards him, drink clutched in hand.

Hello. Ger Philpott, I said holding out my hand.

He nodded with a quizzical look on his face. Cold fish, I thought.

I was Paul's friend, I said. His expression warmed, slightly. Paul talked about you often.

Yes, he said distantly.

Creepy, I thought. He didn't make conversation easy. I drifted away and looked at sailing photographs on the wall. I didn't know most of these people. They all knew each other. I wandered outside to the garden. And sat on the steps of a building beside the house. The sun beat down on my head. Paul would have climbed into one of his grandfather's old suits to come to a party in a house like this, I thought. It was the sort of gathering he would've enjoyed immensely. Why wasn't he here?

How are you doing? Eric asked.

My eyes filled. I'm fine, considering . . . I replied. He touched my shoulder.

Let's go for a walk, he said.

I stood up. Dusted myself down and sighed. Okay, I agreed.

We climbed the wooden fence and walked downhill towards a ditch. The sea was swollen and rushed into the shore below.

Ger, this is just the type of party Paul would've loved, said Eric.

Yes, I was just thinking that, I said fast going off the idea.

What are you going to do now? he asked. I understand that the house in Mount Pleasant Avenue has been let.

That's right. They've put an up-market tenant in. And I'm moving into a dingy flat in Pembroke Lane.

Off Pembroke Road?

No. Off Pembroke Street, I replied.

Here have a drag off this, he said handing me a joint he'd just lit.

I took a toke and handed it back. I'd better not, I said.

We walked back towards the fence and sat on it until it became uncomfortable. Then we went back inside the house. The crowd had thinned somewhat. I joined the people in the conservatory.

I didn't know that Paul and you were so close, his mother said.

What do you mean? Close? I asked. We lived together.

I found some photographs of you both, going through his things. I'd like to keep them.

Bitch, I thought. Of course, I said.

What are you doing now? she asked dismissing me. Audience over. Do you have a lift? The family are going to stay here for a while and then we'll go to the cottage. She turned away before she'd finished speaking.

Don't worry about me, I have a lift. And Denny invited me to join you for supper at the cottage. She was gone.

I couldn't find Eric.

John, are you driving into town? I asked a friend of ours.

Of course. Do you need a lift? I thought the family were staying here, he added, looking at me.

They are. I've been dispatched.

Have lunch with us, we're going to Baggot Lane. To Pat's.

Thank you. I'd like that.

He put his arm around my shoulder and walked me to his car. The second welcome embrace today, I thought. And from another gay man.

Do you have someone to look after you? he asked as we waited for the others to join us.

No. I'll take care of myself, I said looking at the ground.

Be good to yourself. Do you hear? he added insistently.

I nodded.

The other two passengers arrived. Oh good, you're coming to lunch, Pat said. I didn't know what you were doing? He is one of the nicest men I've ever met, I thought. The youngest older man I'd ever known.

How long were you and Paul together? John asked as we drove past the site of the Financial Services Centre. We stopped at the traffic lights near the Custom House.

Four years, I answered, breaking my silence for the first time since we left Jennifer Guinness's house.

That's a long time, they agreed.

I looked, down the river, out to sea as the lights turned green and we drove over the bridge.

* * *

The laughter grew louder as more wine was poured. This was more like a wake, I thought as they swapped stories of Paul.

We went to each other's birthday parties when we were children, said John, one of the guests. It's strange to imagine that he's dead.

I only knew Paul in adult life, said another guest, also called John.

I remember him being naughty and diplomatic, said Pat, our host. Paul was always willing to rescue me when I had to entertain difficult guests.

I sat and listened.

* * *

How did you stay in the church? another guest named John asked me as we strolled in the garden between courses. You're remarkably brave. I thought you'd stab yourself with your chin? It was dug so deep into your chest. It's outrageous that you weren't acknowledged, he added. I intend to take it up with Celestine, he said. I'm meeting him next week. He was referring to the Abbot from Paul's old school.

I listened silently to what he had to say in his sing-song voice.

* * *

I was able to relax with these people, I thought as I spun the large lazy-susan. We whiled the afternoon away around the table in the tiny dining-room.

The doorbell rang.

That must be Denny, said Pat, as he went to answer the door.

So you're here, he intoned; looking in my direction. I didn't know where you were. Are you ready to go to the cottage?

Yes. I rang the flat, but you weren't there, I answered.

Thank you for lunch, Pat. And you've all been very kind. Thank you, I said as we left the drunken lunch party.

Do you have any money? Denny asked as he pulled into a petrol station in Dartry. I need to get petrol.

Here's a tenner, I said handing him a crumpled note. Some things never change. Denny believed that people owed him a living! We drove in silence most of the way.

It's so strange not to have him around, he said. We looked at each other. Sorry, he added as our eyes filled up. I hope this bloody supper is over quickly. Let's make last pints in the Pirate's Den?

That sounds like a great idea, I agreed.

The turf fire was lighting and everyone was busy. The mother. The eldest son. His wife. And her father. The younger son went and pottered in the attic. I climbed the hill behind the cottage. I'd first been here four years ago, I thought. We'd put so much work into the garden. Paul and I. Planting. Cutting grass. Fixing fences. I'll never see it mature now, I thought. I looked at the pattern of woodland across the vast valley.

It grew colder as the sun began to drop in the sky. I noticed a pile of logs outside the garage doors when I came back from my hike. They were begging to be chopped. Made smaller. Hacked to bits. I swung the axe maniacally. I hadn't felt this good all day. Venting my spleen. I went on chopping long after darkness fell. Until I grew afraid to be outside. In the dark.

Supper was supper. I tried unsuccessfully to bring Paul into the conversation. The only reference to him was oblique. That to go to the cottage was preferable to being back in the city. Where people would call and be a disturbance. Denny and I bolted a short while after the meal.

This is one day I'll be glad to see over, he said as we sipped Guinness in the pub on Pembroke Road.

I'm sorry it started, I said. It was too polite for fucking words.

Two pints later we moved on to Jameson whisky. And more whisky. At least the alcohol is comforting, I thought as it warmed my body. Later I cried myself to sleep. The facade down.

★ ★ ★

I was still staying with Denny and got some work in a downstairs flat in his building. I moved the furniture in the sitting-room into the middle of the floor and folded the edges of the carpet in on itself. Paul had been buried for three days at this time. The smell of varnish filled the room as I made my way around painting fresh varnish on the border left by the carpet. The room was dark and *The Gay Byrne Radio Show* played in the background. I began to cry. I stopped painting when my vision blurred and I'd run out of sleeve space to blow my nose. The voices in the other room grew nearer. Shit. The doorknob was turned.

Do you need any more paint stuff? he asked.

It was his flat I was painting. He lived on the ground floor of Denny's building. He was the younger partner of a gay couple who'd given me some work. It was more like occupational therapy. To keep me busy. The money didn't hurt either. This and a few other odd jobs had been offered to me by a couple of concerned gay mafiosi.

I think there's enough, I answered head down to conceal the tears.

Are you okay? . . . Ger, it'll take time. Things will get better, he said soothingly as he closed the door. The *it* that would get better was never mentioned by anyone. *It* had no name.

Later that afternoon I sat on the window-seat in the dining-room at the back of the house, drinking coffee and looking out over the Autumn leaf-strewn garden. Soon the trees will be bare, I thought. The doorbell rang and I heard the key turn in the front door. It was Paul's brothers.

Would you like some coffee? I asked.

Yes, that's very kind of you, the elder one said as Denny nodded. How's the work coming along?

It's almost finished.

What are you doing next?

Some gardening in Baggot Lane, I answered.

The phone bill for Mount Pleasant Avenue has arrived, he said putting the bill on the table. I'm anxious that everything is cleared up quickly.

Let me get my cheque book, I said walking into the hallway to get my back-pack. I concentrated on my handwriting while I slowly wrote the details of the cheque. This is so civilised. Clinical, I thought. I handed him the cheque. He took it from me, pushed his chair away from the table, and stood up.

Can you afford this? he asked as he walked towards

the door. Denny in quick pursuit.

Of course, I said. I heard the door shut as I put the coffee cups in the sink and washed them. This family has the knack of asking *kind* questions on the run, down to a fine art, I thought. I felt shafted.

★ ★ ★

Hello. How are you? he asked.

It was Sean, the man who had driven me to Dublin the first weekend I'd spent with Paul. I was walking down Grafton Street.

Fine, I replied and I started to cry.

What's wrong?

Nothing. Everything, I blurted.

Is Paul giving you a hard time?

I looked into his eyes. He couldn't be joking? I felt he was connected with our lives. I realised he didn't know.

Paul 's dead, I said. The shock came over his face.

I'm sorry, he said. I didn't know.

Are you okay?

No.

I feel awful, he said. I've got to rush to a meeting. What are you doing on Saturday night?

Nothing.

Come to dinner in Patricia's house?

Okay, I replied.

I wasn't sure that I'd go. But on the Saturday night I didn't feel like being alone. My head reeled when I saw that one of the guests, Eimear, had been a guest at dinner in Paul's house, almost the first weekend I'd lived with him. I cooked the meal. Denny was repaying owed hospitality.

I know you from somewhere? Eimear said.

I met you at dinner in Paul's house a few years ago, I explained.

Oh! That's right, he said. How is Paul? The hub-bub of conversation fell around the noisy dinner-table.

He's . . . Paul died about a week ago, I said as the other guests looked away.

The silence grew into a *natural* minute of silence. I had to think about which tense to use. I felt like I imagine a person feels when drowning. Grasping for air.

Where was he buried? he asked breaking the silence.

In Howth last Monday, I said.

I saw a lot of people I knew driving through Sutton that day. And I wondered if somebody gay had died, he said.

I remember thinking that if you'd been there, the way the funeral went and the service it'd have been difficult to know somebody gay had died. It'd have been difficult to know somebody gay had *lived*.

* * *

I went around zombie-like. Physically present. But my mind absent. Elsewhere. I imagined that Paul was still alive. That a dreadful mistake had been made about him being dead. I clung to the hope that he'd round a corner one day. I wanted this to happen sooner than later. I'd already written the script in my head: He'd wandered off somewhere and was suffering from amnesia. He mightn't recognise me when he saw me. But when I'd touch him it would all fall back into place. Our life.

* * *

I can't believe that he's dead, I told my sister Joan. I was visiting her at her house in Swords. She'd suggested that I do my laundry in her house. It was a way of getting me out of myself. Paul had been dead three weeks. We sat opposite each other, warmed by a blazing fire. I fought the tears back.

It must be difficult for you. I can't imagine how you're feeling. You'll just have to pull yourself together and get on with things. I don't know how I'd cope if I were you, she added shaking her head.

I left for the bus before her two sons came home from school. The rain poured heavily as I waited for the bus.

As a child, when it rained, I'd beg my mother to let me walk the dog. I'd eventually set off wrapped up in a raincoat and wellies, having worn her down. I loved being out and about in the rain. It helped me think.

Thoughts of Paul raced through my mind as I stood in the Swords bus shelter. I began to cry. By the time the bus arrived I'd stopped crying. I felt that something was coming up inside me. Falling into place. But, I couldn't work out exactly what. The scenery of Dublin airport and Santry didn't help as the bus made its way into the city. I wanted to be curled up, warm in my bed. I transferred to another bus in O'Connell Street, which stopped on Baggot Street near my flat. I looked through the rain-speckled window at Government Buildings as we drove up Merrion Street. The penny dropped. *I'd never see Paul again*. It was as if a tidal wave had hit me. It was the first time since his death that I understood he'd never again draw breath. And I couldn't understand why it had happened.

By the time I reached the flat I was inconsolable. My absentee flatmate Patsy called to see our new abode.

What's up Philpott? she asked. I was incoherent. She

plied me with gin and tonic in an attempt to get sense out of me. But there wasn't any sense to be got out of me. She drew me a bath into which I climbed gladly. She sat on the toilet seat and topped up my gin and bath water from time to time. I calmed down.

Sorry about the hysterics, I said. Today was the first day I realised that Paul's really dead.

Fuck it, Philpott, you must be in bits, she said as she began to cry. Jesus, now I'll be as bad as you were a few minutes ago. What do you want to do tonight? Do you want to go to the pictures? she asked.

No, I answered.

I'll turn on your blanket and get some food. Would you like some Chinese? I nodded smilingly as she left the bathroom. I rarely eat Chinese food or drink gin and tonic now.

★ ★ ★

I loved listening to the radio. I'd often tried unsuccessfully to ring the shows to comment on the topics being discussed. I wondered if the other people listening in were like me. Alone. The day I realised I was on the brink of ringing the *Gay Byrne Show* to tell him of my aloneness I knew I was in trouble. I had to do something about my life. I devised a strategy. A form of occupational therapy to fill my days. I went to Moore Street and Camden Street markets to buy vegetables each day. I'd go to Bewley's, each afternoon usually, to buy a loaf of coarse wholemeal bread. The littlest thing took on a major significance as I tried to fill my days with rituals.

Bewley's in Grafton Street was a welcome pit-stop for a caffeine and sugar fix after a morning's radio listening and an afternoon's reading in bookshops. I went there a couple of days each week. Amidst the general hustle and bustle, I noticed a group of seven or eight gay men whom I knew. Or was familiar with. They were a loose group. Not exactly the butcher, baker and candlestick-maker. But there was a train-driver, a student of French, a maths lecturer, a professor, a nurse, a rich kid who was perpetually stoned, another who was unemployed and happy to be that way, and an architect. Others came and went. It was a mixed fluid group.

I watched them from a distance at first. I envied their laughter. And camaraderie. They were comfortable with each other. I hadn't known this side of gay life when I was with Paul.

Do you mind if I join you, I asked one day.

Well, Mr High-and-Mighty deigns to joins us, the traindriver said. The others giggled.

Ignore him, Gerry, the maths lecturer said in his lilting Cork tones.

The name's Ger, I said.

Excuse me, said the student of French. And everybody laughed. They were easy company. There was a lot of banter and gossip. They chatted about films and theatre. Exhibitions and current affairs also featured as did who bonked whom at the weekend.

I joined the group a couple of afternoons each week. Sometimes it was hard to pull myself out of the doldrums. But it helped when I did. They made no demands. They were a lifeline.

Some of the group have already died from AIDS. Others are HIV positive.

★ ★ ★

I went to Cork a month after Paul's death. My parents wanted me to visit sooner. But I didn't go earlier because I was afraid that I might've stayed there. Fallen back into the womb, so to speak. I felt strange about going back because it would mean admitting that Paul had died. Sometimes my immediate family asked how I was but, apart from that, nobody brought up the fact that Paul had died. Except my sister-in-law, Bernice. This suited me fine. Yet I wanted people to talk about what happened. Because I needed to be recognised. The contradiction of my feelings was baffling. If people couldn't deal with Paul's death, then I was alone. To gloss over the initial awkward silences when I met people. People took their cues from me.

* * *

It was a Thursday night. A popular night out in any university city. Loafers, Cork's gay bar, was no exception. I could see a crowd gathered inside through the frosted glass on the door. I drew a deep breath as I turned the doorknob. The owner, an old friend, was behind the bar. We looked into each other's eyes.

Ger, how are you? I was sad to hear about Paul's death. Are you all right? he asked.

Thank you. I'm fine, I said, thinking – please hold me.

What will you have to drink?

A pint of Murphys please.

It's on me, he said when I offered him money for the drink.

Thanks.

I'll come out to chat when my relief comes on duty, he said.

I nodded and smiled.

I saw them when I turned from the bar. Two gay politicos, men I'd hung out with before I met Paul, were sitting under the window at a corner table. Our eyes met briefly and then they looked at the ground. I halted, more in my mind than in my stride. How are you? I asked pulling a stool from underneath the table as I joined them.

When did you come down? the one who had been my lover asked.

Two days ago, I answered.

How long are you down for? asked the other.

Till Saturday, I replied. Later we were joined by some other people. Nobody mentioned Paul's death. It was as if he'd never died. Never lived. Business as usual in the watering hole.

* * *

Fuck them, they're pathetic, I thought as I walked home. All talk and no shagging action. I felt utterly betrayed. They didn't ask me how I was. Why hadn't they asked me about Paul's death?

It was obvious from the way they looked at me that they knew Paul had died. Even the pillars of gay political Cork didn't have the courage to help me, I thought as I stopped for chips near Parliament Bridge.

My friend Patsy was in Cork that weekend. I saw her the following Monday evening.

Kieran and Arthur were asking for you at the weekend. They wanted to know if you were coping okay, she said.

It's a pity they didn't think of asking me directly on Thursday when I was in Loafers, I replied.

What! They didn't talk about it when you met them? she asked.

I shook my head in response.

Their politics must be up their arses, not to mention common decency, she replied. We looked at each other and broke into laughter.

Cork sucks. But at least it's got Murphys going for it, I said.

Yeah, it has to have some redeeming features, she said as we giggled.

* * *

One evening when I was in Cork I had dinner with a married couple I was friendly with. They'd met Paul. They were very kind and made all the right noises. But I felt that nobody really understood. I didn't understand what was going on with me either. And it annoyed me when people said that time would heal the pain. How did they know? What pain were they talking about? When had their partners died? I left Cork feeling more alone than ever. I was glad I was going back to Dublin. Whatever kind of life I had there it would be infinitely better than any I could've had in Cork.

I'd hoped going to Cork would help me deal with Paul's death. It didn't. There were no quick-fix solutions available. It was clear that I'd have to do all the work myself. People's silences were insensitive. I believe now that people did the best they could. But I was less forgiving at the time.

I was the bereft partner in a gay relationship. So people who knew me had to think about how they saw gay relationships. Their validity and worthwhileness. I couldn't help knowing that things would have been different if I was heterosexual and had lost my partner . . .

I felt strange sitting in the train as it climbed through the tunnel out of Cork's Kent Station. This is the longest and steepest railway tunnel in Europe, I remembered being told once.

Chapter Seven

I stayed in Denny's flat for a week after Paul died. A friend gave me a message from a gay doctor, Dermot Roche. Paul and I, along with half the gay population of Dublin, knew him professionally. Dermot had passed on his condolences and asked me to come and see him if I needed any help. I was finding it very difficult to sleep at this stage. A stiff drink would knock me out but I'd be awake within a few hours and toss and turn for the rest of the night. I decided to visit Dermot's surgery on the Saturday morning after Paul's funeral to get some sleeping tablets. I thought I'd go crazy if I didn't get a good night's sleep.

I heard on the radio that morning that Dermot had died in a plane crash in Wales. His small airplane hit a fog-covered mountain. The one person I felt I could talk to was now also dead. I took this to mean that sleeping tablets were not for me.

My new flat was on Pembroke Lane around the corner from the Pembroke bar on Pembroke Street. I moved in a week after Paul's burial. It was over a garage in an old mews house at the back of 55 Fitzwilliam Square. The street door was a grey-blue colour. Inside, a narrow rickety stairs led to my flat door and to another unoccupied flat behind mine.

The flat was like a series of small railway carriages.

Long and narrow. The flat door opened on to a corridor. You couldn't swing a cat in the tiny-windowed kitchen. Two steps, up a short passage, led to the bathroom and one of the bedrooms. The living-room was about ten feet long and eight feet wide. The selling point of the flat was the big picture window in the living-room. It gave a lot of light to the otherwise dark flat. The second bedroom was at the end of the living-room. This was the biggest room in the flat. It overlooked the street. It had the advantage of being the full width of the building. It overhung the stairs that climbed from the street to my flat door.

The flat had no furniture worth speaking of. It was dull and dirty. I bought furniture at auctions – beds, bentwood chairs, carpets, kitchen cupboards and an Art Deco wardrobe. I painted the walls with white emulsion and the floors with red floor paint. I made a roman blind for the living-room window with grey and white mattress ticking. I painted the bentwood chairs battleship grey. My prize possession was an eighteenth century occasional table, in need of repair. Paul had bought it from Travellers on the road to Wicklow for me. Painting the flat took about two weeks to finish.

I threw myself into fixing up the flat and got through the days with ample supplies of wine and gin, which I stole from a nearby off-licence. I had a large overcoat. I wore the coat with one sleeve stuffed with a jumper and kept my arm free on the inside for the shoplifting-spree. I would use the free hand to grab the booze and hold it inside the coat while I finished the shopping and went to pay. It was unnerving at first. I'd chat to the person at the till while I kept an awkward grip on the bottles. I became expert at this method of getting booze. Sometimes I'd have a bottle stashed in each of the coat's deep pockets and another grasped in my hand. I was never caught – even when I was brazen about the theft. At one point I brought some friends, who were curious about my stash of alcohol, to see my modus operandi. It was a great source of amusement.

My career as a petty thief was an attempt to attract attention. I *wanted* to be caught because I'd have been the centre of attention then instead of being isolated. I had several callers during this period. Friends I'd met through Paul. They called to see that I was okay. Some of them thought taking care of me involved more than I was prepared to give. They stopped calling when I didn't respond to their advances.

Twelve days after Paul died I was near breaking point. That night I couldn't face being alone. I decided to go out. I went downtown. I thought of the Petula Clarke song of the same name *Downtown* as I walked along Merrion Row. The song always conjured up childhood memories of crowds awaiting the arrival of the stars outside the Savoy cinema in Cork during Film Festival week. Not so glamorous now, I thought, as I headed towards St Stephen's Green.

Outside the Shelbourne Hotel I thought about the University church, directly across the green, where Paul's funeral was held less than two weeks before. It was better to be out and about with my thoughts than at home with them. I didn't know exactly where I was going. I walked up and down streets for a couple of hours and eventually decided that I'd go to a gay bar.

I went to the Viking on Dame Street. I was scared and fragile. It felt like the first time I went into a gay bar. I ordered a pint and sat on a dais near the exit. I drank my pint trying to look preoccupied. This was difficult. There was nothing to focus on, apart from the tacky carpet and the wrought-iron sections between seats. I was sure the people who were looking at me were gossiping: That's the guy who went out with Denny's brother. He died two weeks ago. They say he had some kind of cancer.

So I imagined their conversations. I left the bar after a second drink because I felt too self-conscious. I didn't want to go home. I headed for Bartley Dunnes. Another gay bar. On my way home. I didn't want to be alone.

The bar was dark. There was another hour's drinking left and the last drinks crowd hadn't yet arrived. I passed the alcoves opposite the bar and went to the back and ordered a pint. I looked at the framed pictures of Hollywood Greats on the walls. nobody interesting about. Nobody I knew. I suddenly panicked. Catholic guilt, no doubt. Here I was out. Cruising. And Paul not yet cold in his grave. Yet, I could keep it together in the bar. It was the first evening for a while that I hadn't cried. I decided to stay and have another pint. The alcohol was now taking effect, its warmth spreading inside me.

I walked down the bar towards the front door. I always felt that only hopeless cases did this. A final attempt to scan the bar for a possible partner to spend the night with. A sure sign of being hard up. I'd never really liked gay bars. But my opinion of them was changing rapidly. I felt secure. Nobody was going to hassle me. And I wasn't at home alone. I walked to the other end of the bar. I would leave when I finished my pint. He caught my eye as I neared the door. He looked eagerly at me. He was tall. Dark. And wore glasses. I turned and ordered another pint. I wasn't quite sure how I was going to do what I was about to do. I'd never had difficulty meeting people. Usually, I'd decide whether I wanted them or not. I was now, it seemed, about to pick up a stranger.

I stood at the bar working out what I'd say – Hi. How are you, my name's Ger. Or. What's your name? Mine's Ger – Really what I wanted to say was: come home with me. Take care of me.

I took my pint and nodded to him as I went towards the wall he leaned against. The barman called last drinks. His glass was practically empty. Shit. He smiled at me as he passed. Yes, he was ordering another drink. He came back from the bar and stood against the wall. We were about three places apart from each other. It seemed like an eternity until I half-turned in his direction.

I don't come here very often. But I felt like a drink tonight and decided to come here. Do you come here often? he said.

He was beside me. I turned fully and looked at him. He was very attractive. Big. Not unlike Christopher Reeves. I wondered if he turned into Superman when he took the glasses off.

No, I hardly ever come here. Usually, I'm with friends, I answered.

My name is David, he said.

We looked each other up and down. What the fuck am I doing? I asked myself. There was something gentle about him. We both finished our drinks at the same time. He offered to get more drinks. We both had gin and tonics. The seats in the nearby alcove were free so we sat down.

I've just moved into to a flat nearby. I've been painting all day and came out for a breather, I offered.

I was training and dropped in here on the way home on the off-chance there'd be someone interesting here. I'd about given up hope until I saw you walking out, he replied.

We both smiled. Me with relief. This guy was making picking him up very easy.

Bartley Dunnes was notorious for the crackling tannoy request to clear the premises. We made our way out to the street as the noise clamoured around us. I accepted a lift home. The flat looked shitty. I gave him the quick guided tour and poured two gin and tonics. We chatted away about this, that and the other.

I wanted to ask him to have sex with me. But couldn't get it together. I was in a state of paralysis. Not because of the alcohol. Because of the guilt.

Do you think we could, perhaps, explore your bedroom? he asked, three gin and tonics later.

Lois Lane eat your heart out. I broke down as dawn approached and told him about Paul. He was very loving.

Can I see you again? he asked, as he left.

Yes, I'd like that, I answered. I curled up in the warm sheets and drifted back to sleep.

David didn't call the next day. Or the day after. Or the day after that. I felt used but steeled myself. I was finding it very difficult to sleep at night. I got used to the idea that my evening with David was only a casual fling. Two weeks later, at about six-thirty, my doorbell rang. I was taken aback to see David at the door.

I'm sorry I didn't call before now. And I was wondering if you'd like to have a drink this evening? David said.

Yes, I'd like that, I replied.

About two months into our relationship David and I happened to be driving down Mount Pleasant Avenue.

I slept with a guy who lived in that house, David said as we passed number 9.

I couldn't believe what I'd heard.

Stop and let's go for a drink, I said a few moments later, as we drove over Rathmines bridge.

We sat at the bar in Searsons drinking.

Describe the guy you slept with who lived in Mount Pleasant avenue, I asked casually.

He was tall and very passionate, said David.

What was his name? I asked.

I think it was Peter or Paul. I'm not sure. It was a couple of years ago, and it was only a one-night stand, David replied. Why're you so interested ?

That's the house I lived in with Paul. You slept with Paul when I was living with him, I said. I'm not getting at you for being with him, I added. It's just that of all the people in Dublin that I end up dating, don't you think it's strange that it should be you? I can't believe it, I kept repeating.

Later that night as we made love I was torn between being with David and fantasising about being with Paul. And David together.

I believed that David had come along as Paul's replacement. He had the same background. His father even once worked in the same field as Paul's. We had a very physical relationship. That was important because I needed not to feel alone. We were together for two years. We argued a lot. Mainly because David was in the closet. David was a six-foot-four former rower. Built, as they say, like a brick shithouse. Not the stereotypical gay man. His job meant that he had to attend a lot of functions to which I wasn't invited. I goaded him about this.

Not because I wanted to go to the boring functions but because I thought it was ridiculous that he was in the closet. He'd arrange to call to my flat after the events. He was always late and I'd get in a stew. The rows that followed became so ritual that it was like foreplay. He arrived drunk at my flat one evening after a dinner. I'd seen him earlier that evening, walking into a city hotel with a woman on his arm. She was a PR person whom he knew. She was obviously his date for the evening.

How was the do?

It was fine, the usual boring work stuff, David answered.

Anyone there that I know ?

No I don't think so, he said.

What was Sally doing with you?

How do you know she was there ?

I saw her walking into the hotel with you on my way home from the pool, I said.

Ger, I have to have a date for these things, that's the way it's done, he answered.

And it's written in stone somewhere that the date has to be of the opposite sex?

It's easier for me that way, he replied.

I was annoyed about this. Not because he was with a woman. But because he lied about it. Closeted gay people find it very easy to lie about things like this. It's second nature for them. They spend a lifetime denying their sexuality. To cover up for the double lives they lead. I can understand why; given the society we live in. It's insulting to people who are out.

We argued also because I made a lot of demands. It was a confusing time. I felt the need to be in the relationship rather than not. I don't think I could have survived without it. I needed a David desperately. He kept me from thinking about Paul. Being with David allowed me to put my grief on hold.

* * *

I processed my grief through a system of controlled slow release. Very controlled. I couldn't consciously deal with what had happened. Nobody gave me support. It was a question of get on with your life. Put this ordeal behind you. I felt isolated. I knew no one who had gone through what I'd experienced. And felt angry when people said time would heal the pain. They were trying to tell me to get over it. Saying : Don't annoy me with this.

David was a baby in emotional terms. There was never a question of pouring out my heart to him. I *needed* to be with David as often as possible. Daytime wasn't too bad. We spent most nights together. I'd allow myself to think about Paul when I was with David. Often imagining I was with Paul and not David. As a result I was passionate beyond the potential of our relationship. It was a fair trade. David was having the time of his life.

Will you get *The Irish Times*, I asked one rainy Saturday morning. I'll make breakfast, I added encouragingly.

No.

Come on. Why not?

I don't want to get up yet, he smiled.

I laughed as he climbed under the duvet.

Hmmm. He put up a good argument. The newspaper could wait.

I couldn't get Paul out of my head. Now and then I'd take some of my feelings out and deal with them. But often more than I could deal with came up. I had to keep things together to stay sane. David and I argued a lot but it wasn't that bad. We always made up and that was good. For a while.

* * *

I celebrated New Year's Eve, 1983, with David, Paul's brother Denny, and his boyfriend Colm.

We met in the Viking bar, had a few drinks and went to David's house in Lombard Street West to see in the New Year. We smoked a joint. David popped champagne. St Patrick's Cathedral's bells rang in the New Year. We toasted each other and kissed as the countdown ended. I noticed Denny looking at me when Colm was hugging him and David hugging me. There was no need to say anything. The look said it all.

He's a nice guy. You're right to take care of yourself, Denny said to me later in a nightclub.

* * *

Winter deepened and the roof of the flat leaked. I was still finding it difficult to sleep at night, especially when David wasn't there. The sound of the rain dripping into a basin at the foot of my bed, didn't help either. Often on these nights I'd get up and walk. Walk along the beach in Sandymount and sometimes get as far as the pier in Dun Laoghaire. I'd work out scenarios in my head. About how I'd sort out my life. I thought a lot about marriage at the time. How settling down would give me the security that I needed. The obvious solution, I thought, to my problems was to move back to Cork and marry a lesbian woman I knew.

I fantasised about opening a stripped furniture shop in Cork's Wintrop Street. I'd picked out the premises. A small shop opposite the Long Valley. Working out the details of the shop, suppliers, sales potential etc helped me stay sane. It was bitterly cold, often, but I'd wrap myself up in the plans and logistics as the wind howled around me. Anything to avoid lying awake in bed.

It didn't work. I began swimming again. The exercise made me tired and gradually I began to fall into more regular sleeping patterns. To this day sleeplessness remains one of my worst nightmares.

* * *

I met Kay Sheehy, and later her sister Joan, during the summer of the 1983 anti-amendment campaign. We were in the same action group. I wasn't as active as the Sheehy women. But we became good friends. People worked hard during the campaign. But it wasn't all work. We also played hard. It was an exciting time.

Kay was a dynamic force. I was impressed with her grasp of politics. She was an able clever woman. She was also blonde and dizzy. I loved her appetite for fun.

We were immediate friends. And kindred spirits. She'd replace the Bible on my desert island. Every day.

Kay and Joan never got the chance to meet Paul because he was hospitalised when we met. I received two condolence cards after Paul's death, one from my childhood friend Annette in Cork and the other from Kay.

Kay's card – an Impressionistic picture of two boys on a beach – reminded me of a childhood photograph of my brothers and sister taken in Youghal where we spent our holidays.

After I met David for the first time, and before our affair, Kay and I went out together one Saturday evening. I was having a rough time and Kay's suggestion to go out was a godsend. Kay called to my flat and we were having a drink when, out of the blue, I broke down.

I'm sorry about this Kay I said, but I feel like I'm going crazy. All this stuff is going on in my head. I can't stop thinking about Paul. I feel like it's a terrible mistake and that he'll turn up and everything will be all right, I added.

We were sitting in the living-room of my flat. Kay was in the armchair and I sat at her feet.

It was very cold and we were huddled against the two-bar electric heater. I began to cry.

What was Paul like? Kay asked.

I talked for a while. I don't remember exactly what I said. But, after a while, I realised I had to stop talking and crying. Too much was coming up and if I didn't bottle things up, I was going to lose control.

The following May I moved flat. A bed-sit was free in the house where Kay and Joan Sheehy lived on Fitzwilliam Place. I lived overhead, their bed-sits were below.

The house was largely unoccupied and the three of us had great fun wandering about the rooms of the lower floors acting out scenarios amidst the French painted regency furniture. Around the same time that I moved, I got a job as a lifeguard with Dublin Corporation. I was stationed at Sean McDermott St pool.

★ ★ ★

More information and discussion about AIDS hit the media that Spring. I allowed myself wonder again about Paul's death. I read an American magazine article on the effects of AIDS. Paul's symptoms and decline from good health read like a textbook case-history of the disease. Somehow

I could accept this idea. It was inevitable, I thought, that I too would have the disease. This was mid-1984. I was beginning to understand that there was very little you could do about AIDS. So I played a waiting game.

* * *

I met an Australian named Anthony with his boyfriend, David, on a visit to Cork that Summer. Even though he was with his boyfriend, he made it very obvious that he was interested in me. I found the attention exciting.

I'm going to be in Dublin next week. I'd like to get together with you if you'd like, Anthony asked.

What about your boyfriend? I asked.

We've an open relationship, he replied.

We agreed that he'd call me the following Tuesday. I looked forward to that, and when he phoned, we arranged that Anthony would come to supper in my flat. He arrived about nine-thirty. Kay joined us for supper and later we went to the pub for a drink.

Back in the flat, Anthony explained that if we were going to sleep together we'd have to have safe sex. Up to that point I associated safe sex with not getting a woman pregnant.

What's safe sex? I asked, somewhat amused.

Anthony explained that it was a way of not picking up diseases. You wouldn't exchange body fluids and as a result you'd avoid AIDS.

I'd never thought of sex as an exchange of body fluids. I always believed that good sex was about a meeting of minds. Anthony's strategy made it sound like pass-the-parcel. There'd be no wet kissing. You had to keep your mouth closed. There'd be no penetration. No oral sex. Just sealed-lip kissing, hugging and mutual masturbation. Before this gay sex was all about getting the ride. Fucking. Anthony was opening up new possibilities! I must admit that I found the whole procedure a little strange, if not frustrating. It was very tantalising; desiring his tongue in my mouth. And other things. No way. Anthony was resolute. The excitement and anticipation was, however, rewarding. Sensationally so. When Anthony left two days later I wasn't too impressed with his green-cross code for sex. But it made me think.

David had been on holidays during Anthony's visit. When he came back I told him about this safe sex thing. We both thought it silly. We agreed that we both liked fucking too much to give it up.

Why don't we try condoms? David suggested.

He'd never used a condom before. He'd never slept with a woman. Whereas I had had a quite successful heterosexual career, one that didn't always involve condom use, I must admit. The novelty of condom use wore off after a few packs. Not to mention the annoyance of discovering the shagging things had ripped during use. It wasn't until a full year later that I really began to practice safe sex. But Anthony from Australia sowed the seed of thoughts that would ultimately shape my future.

* * *

I had dinner with David in New York three years later. I was visiting a boyfriend and David was working there temporarily. We went to a gay restaurant.

You were very important for me at the time following Paul's death, I told him.

He was dismissive about this.

No, it's important for me to say this. I don't think I would've survived without your being there for me, I added.

Later David walked me back to where I was staying.

We did everything together didn't we? David said, outside the door of the apartment.

How do you mean? I asked.

Sexually. We did everything? David was very uptight about AIDS at this point. I've been celibate for more than a year, he said. I'm paranoid about AIDS. Now, I don't do anything. I bet you're doing everything with the guy you're visiting, David added. I looked at him, smiled. Yes, I said.

We kissed awkwardly and he left. I haven't seen him since.

* * *

I decided to move back to Cork in the Autumn of 1984. I spent the previous Winter, Spring and Summer licking my wounds. I put a certain shape back into my life but the truth was that Dublin was proving too much for me to handle.

There were too many ghosts from the past. I kept running into familiar situations. The last time I'd done these things, been to these places, I was with Paul. Stopping for a drink in a country pub. Going to a concert. Seeing a re-run of a movie on TV. The list went on and on and seemed like it would never end.

I'm moving back to Cork this September, I told the man who drove me to the flower market the day of Paul's funeral when I met him outside the Kildare St gates of the Dail.

Is that wise? he asked.

There are too many variables that I don't control here. I know it's a bit like running away. But it'll be much easier to manage things down south, I said.

Chapter Eight

The smell from Patrick's Bridge is wick-et. How do Fa-der Mat-chew stick it? How'd I stick it was more relevant. Cork's a place where the rain is tor-i-enchal and the inhabitants are fed, daily, two doses of introspection in the form of the *Cork Examiner* and the *Evening Echo*. I'd felt, growing up in Cork, that something was always pissing down on top of me. Less travelling backward and more like a pit-stop. To live in Cork again was like exile in the home-town. I've a love-hate relationship with the place.

My belongings were packed into the carrier on the roof of David's Volkswagen Golf. I looked out over the reclaimed land, that is now part of Cork's industrial harbour to the left side of the road as we drove into the city from Dunkettle Bridge. And remembered my childhood fascination when my father told the story about Dutch workers who built the polders there.

I remember the silvery waterlogged polders, divided and plotted, their thicket fences in silhouette. They were the final signpost for home at the end of family outings on grey Sunday evenings. Home just a few minutes away. Now, the landscape is an eyesore of oil terminal offices and ferryports. Transformed.

I couldn't make sense of reclamation as a child. There was an elusive magic about it. My return to Cork was an effort to get in touch with some of that childish innocence.

Thainig long o Valparaiso . . . I looked down the river from the bridge at City Hall. It was one of my favourite childhood views. It offered the possibility of escape. Openness. A safe harbour for the clutter of fishing trawlers berthed there during storms. I was now seeking that kind of refuge. It was a gamble. I'd spent most of my life fighting against Cork's parochialism. And now I'd moved back.

I stayed for a while with my aunt, in Blarney Street, a couple of doors down the road from my parents. My family wanted me to live with them. But I'd other ideas. I found a flat on Cork's Wellington Road six weeks after moving back to Cork.

A top floor flat in a large, northside, Victorian building. The building belonged to a friend's relative. It was larger than I needed. With the usual complement of rooms. I liked its spectacular views and the deep clawfooted bath. The bathroom's bay window showed the terraced back garden off to spectacular effect in Spring and Summer. The bathroom was down one flight of stairs atop the building's wooden return.

Cork is shaped like a saucer. Surrounded by hills. I liked the sense of being able to overlook the city from my flat. It gave me the feeling of not being hemmed-in. An all-too-frequent experience for this prodigal son. The wood-panelled living-room was a bit brown for my liking. But it had an open fireplace. What it lacked in brightness, however, it more than made up for with views. The living-room's two windows offered the panorama of Cork's docklands, the harbour, the river Lee and the sweep across the south side of the city, to the encircling foothills in the distance. Sunsets fell through the roof's western window. And the moon made the odd appearance.

I blew some money my parents gave me on a Marantz stereo system. And a few nights on the town. I was now set up: my own pad and great sounds. I worked part-time in a bar, and taught literacy and numeracy, voluntarily, two evenings a week in a working-class northside suburb. With swimming training three times a week on top of that, I'd little spare time. The hectic schedule left little time to think. Exactly what I wanted. I also did some teaching hours in my old Alma Mater, the North Monastery.

Did I mention that going back to Cork was about regression?

Whoever said schooldays are the best days of your life got it wrong. My "Mon" schooldays were the most boring of my life. It wasn't much different as a teacher. Many of the teaching staff were past pupils. "Mon" boys. They went to UCC. And came back to teach. They never grew up. Yes, they probably picked up a wife etc along the way, but little else changed. Each day when I met these teachers I was reminded of the type of teacher I didn't want to be. Lazy and boring.

School for me as a youngster was like running a gauntlet. It was macho beyond belief. I hated it. I figured if I survived those days I'd certainly get over my bereavement.

I loved teaching and regretted I hadn't more teachers like me: Interesting. But for a group of six or so classmates who were great fun, my schooldays in the "Mon" would've been futile. The five-roomed all-Irish secondary school to which I belonged had about one hundred and fifty students at any given time. It attempted to breed arrogance and superiority in its pupils. We were regarded as the academic elite. And were seen as the best bets to get to university. All because of our alleged brains and ability to speak Irish. We'd many privileges. We'd wear army jackets and denim jeans. Exam classes were permitted to study in class at night. Presumably, because the-powers-that-be felt that our working-class homes weren't conducive to study. How's that for apartheid?

One advantage of teaching there was the fact that I could walk up and down the main driveway. This was forbidden as a pupil. I met a demon from my past on the drive one day. A so-called Christian Brother, Lee, who'd taught us. I remembered his brutality. And his dog-breath. His nickname was Sniffs. He was given the name because of his habit of cocking his head and nose in the air. Not unlike the poses adopted by those celebrities photographed in *Hello!* magazine to avoid displaying double-chins. He was a snob.

I literally bumped into him one day. Traces of terror bubbled to the surface. I remembered all the beatings he'd given me. And others. If that happened today, the bollocks would be locked up for abuse. I remembered him reading the riot act one morning following an incident with geranium plants. My older brother, Ted's, class was studying in school after hours. That particular evening it rained. Rather than go to the outside toilets, one of my brother's mates, Pius, pissed in the geraniums, decorating the BVM's altar.

The next morning the plants were dead and Sniffs was on the warpath. He stormed into my brother's classroom and demanded to be told what had happened to the plants. There was silence.

Who killed the geraniums? he asked the guy who'd pissed on them.

Pius cracked up. Quickly followed by the entire class. Word had spread and soon the pupils from the other classes were peering through the windows of the corridors and the partitions between classrooms; laughing. Sniffs Nil. Pupils One.

I usually dropped into my parent's house for coffee after my morning class. I told my mother the geranium story and my encounter with the demon monk on the drive.

The day our Leaving Certificate exams were over, I sent umpteen taxis from different companies to the school for Sniffs. The taxis were to arrive at five-minute intervals, I told her. Can you imagine what his anxiety levels must've been as taxi after taxi called to the monastery's residence looking for Brother Lee? I said.

A pathetic schoolboy prank, my mother said as we laughed.

I suppose I should be grateful that he stopped at beatings. Other Brothers made pathetic attempts at sexual molestation.

* * *

By the time I'd reached Cork I was a six-foot-two beanpole weighing just under ten stone. I'd lived on my nerves during Paul's illness and had lost over two stone. I was told afterwards that the first night I went to the swimming-pool for training people couldn't believe that I'd have the strength to swim to the other end of the pool. The pool was a natural a haven for me, as it was when I worked out adolescent turmoils about being gay. I thrived. Out of, yet in, my element. Swimming length after length.

When you focus on breath and stroke technique some coping strategy kicks in. Stress disappears. I can't imagine not swimming.

Master's swimming is like age-group swimming for adults. It goes up in five-year bands beginning at age twenty-five. My parents and many childhood friends were involved. I decided to swim competitively again. Swimming became my opium. I never missed a training session in Cork over the next three years.

I dedicated, pompously and idealistically, my efforts and accomplishments to Paul and the pursuit of fitness and health. Memories of Paul were more manageable in Cork. It was good to get away from the scenes of our life together. I was free to think of him. And what my own life added up to. I felt like no one else I knew.

* * *

I loved being near my younger brother's two kids. He now has four children. They're adorable. The boys were great fun and close companions. A little more than a year between them, these two bright-eyed blonds were practically edible. They'd come to my flat and stay. Jamie, the elder, was four at the time. I'd a low-lying bed, futon-style, on the floor of my bedroom. The boys played pillow-fights one Saturday morning; clambered over my bed trying to wake me up. I got them to settle for a less vigorous activity. I turned on the television.

Padraig, the younger of the two, became engrossed in the telly. Jamie as usual asked questions. I was still half-asleep.

Why don't you have a colour telly? Don't you have a video? Do you like living on your own? he asked.

Usually, I replied.

Will you take us to the swimming-pool today? he asked.

Okay, I said.

Ger, when did your wife die? was his next question.

Where is he coming from with this, I thought, as I sat up and looked at him. Padraig's attention had now strayed from the television to us.

I've never been married, Jamie, I answered.

Yes you were, and your wife died. I heard my mom and dad talking about it, he said.

So did I, Padraig added.

I'm afraid you picked it up wrong, I answered. My friend Paul died. We weren't married, I told them.

My story was being rewritten. But what do you tell a couple of kids? The re-invention revealed a multitude. The boy's mother, Bernice, for whom I've great admiration told me, on my return to Cork, that she was sorry about Paul's death. That was good to hear. Other acknowledgements came through looks. Safe looks. Looks I'd to decipher. The unspoken message was pick yourself up and get on with it. I'd difficulty with this. What was I supposed to pick myself up *from*?

It was important that I'd be confronted with the *fact* of Paul's death. If for no other reason than to make my mourning real. Banishment to the ranks of the unspoken may have made it easier for the silent, but it was a fat lot of use to me. It was as if he'd never existed. As if *we* never existed. I didn't talk about it either. I felt robbed. There was one thing, however, no one could take away from me. Our love. I relived every detail of it over and over again in my head. That was my sanity.

116

* * *

My relationship with David had, effectively, petered out by this point. We saw each other from time to time. Long-distance relationships don't work for me. I restarted a friendship with a lesbian woman.

The duck-a-l'orange led to finger licking. And then . . . Later, we lay entwined, breathless, on the living-room floor.

What are we doing? she asked.

You mean is this for real? I countered.

Let's get married, she said.

We looked at each other. It certainly appealed to our sense of the subversive.

Okay, let's do it, I said.

We laughed about it being Cork's wedding of the year. The relationship could never have succeeded. Because we both pretended it wasn't happening in the first place. I'd been back in Cork a year at this point. Instead of getting married in August as we'd joked, I headed to Canada to swim in the inaugural World Masters Games. My parents came too, with a group of twenty-five Cork swimmers.

After the Games my folks and I headed to New York. They to visit relatives. Me to lose myself on the streets of Manhattan. We drove from Toronto to Buffalo in upstate New York to catch a cheap People's Express flight to Newark Airport. On the way we stopped off at Niagara Falls. I enjoyed the trip. But I couldn't help thinking how strange it was to be at one of the world's cliched honeymoon venues with my parents. I spent the first night with my folks in dad's brother's house in New Jersey. Then I headed for the city. I'd stayed downtown, on the Lower Eastside. It was great to be back in New York. I got in touch with Loring, a friend's old college-mate. We went to see Sam Sheppards *Curse of the Working Class* at an upper West Side theatre. There were live sheep on stage. Loring bought the theatre tickets and I bought dinner after the show. We ate sushi and drank Heineken. We poured our hearts out to each other. It was romantic. We were both in search of the big L . . .

I don't know anyone who's had that experience. It must've been awful for you, he said when I told him about Paul.

I needed to hear those words. We discussed AIDS in detail. He was the first person that I'd spoken with about the AIDS theory and Paul's death. He was familiar with AIDS in New York. The type of reality that hadn't yet hit Ireland. For most people.

I was anxious to glean as much information as I could from him. I felt vulnerable as we headed in different directions to catch our respective trains. I wondered if he found me attractive.

* * *

I went back to Cork and began teaching in Colaiste Mhuire, a co-ed convent school in Cobh, outside the city. I also had a part-time job as an assistant health education officer attached to the Southern Health Board. The Health Board job involved talking about health to community groups. My friend Mary McGrath worked there too. The brief was broad and we were allowed to decide about programme development. We both had frustrating experiences about what were referred to as "sensitive issues". Mary wanted to get a speaker from a family planning clinic to speak to a group of women. I wanted to start an AIDS education initiative.

It won't go down well with the powers that be, advised our immediate boss. I'm behind you but you'll end up losing your jobs, she said.

So much for support. And this was 1985.

* * *

The World Health Organisation sponsored a medical conference in Trinity College that winter. Two doctors from San Francisco were delegates at the conference. They'd spoken on the *Morning Ireland* radio programme. About AIDS and the threat it posed in America. Both doctors were gay. Around this time a number of gay men in Dublin and Cork had started to meet to discuss the AIDS threat. These groups became known as Gay Health Action. I went to the Cork meetings. This was the first positive response to AIDS in Ireland. All subsequent organisations evolved from that first handful of gay men.

The Californian doctors organised a course. It was held at the JCR in Trinity the weekend following the WHO conference. I went with two other gay politicos from Cork. There were about fifteen men, all gay, at the workshop. The workshop began with a general discussion of the planned format. The doctors, Glenn and Jon, asked for a commitment from everyone that they'd stay with the workshop for the duration.

They explained they worked with the Shanti Project in San Francisco. The project helped people with AIDS by providing "buddies". The "buddy" became the person's support and helped him. The workshop began with a video about HIV testing and slides of people, men, with AIDS. These were like the horrible pictures of diseased body parts you see in medical textbooks. I sat there transfixed. Put Paul's head on those images . . . his body had looked exactly like that. The gauntness. The hairlessness. The sores on the body. Above all, the big staring eyes peculiar to people close to death. Paul was a textbook example of clinical manifestations of AIDS. I couldn't deny it anymore.

After the movies we sat in a circle and talked about how we felt and why we'd come to the workshop.

The video and slides have confirmed my lover died of AIDS, was my offering. I then talked about how I'd denied this for the past two years. I felt a rush of adrenalin while I spoke – as If I was playing sports.

But this wasn't about playing. I was scared. Especially having heard what they'd to say about the disease being sexually transmitted. I'm fucked, I thought. Not to mention the people I've slept with since Paul died. I hadn't even worn condoms when I'd slept with women. I was cruising for a bruising in terms of guilt.

I returned reluctantly to the workshop the next morning. I was a bit uneasy. But my thirst for information won out. Anyway I'd given a commitment to carry it through. Part of the day's activities was a death simulation exercise. Jon and Glenn bored on about light at the end of the tunnel before death.

It was important that potential "buddies" would've some experience of this before they talked to someone with AIDS, they said.

The group lay down, waiting to be guided through the death simulation exercise. I felt hot. And bothered. It was a bit too close for comfort. I felt that I couldn't back out. I lay there and listened to the instructions, conscious of the other people in the room.

Paul died alone in a hospital bed. When I last saw him alive he was agitated and upset. I imagine he died distraught; feeling abandoned. My biggest problem about his death was the fact that he died alone. That I wasn't with him. I hadn't learned to cope with this particular ghost at the time of the workshop. As I entered my particular tunnel of death there was no light. Just darkness. The others were talked through their journeys to the warmth and the light at the end of their respective tunnels, mine grew darker and darker. Virtual reality. I made sounds. Battled to keep my tears and cries silent. It was no use. I broke down and bawled my heart out. I didn't understand why I'd let this happen to me.

Two people from the group moved close to me. One held my hand, the other stroked my head. I felt violated by their nearness. I wanted them to disappear off the face of the earth. But I couldn't do anything about it. I realised that they'd stay as long as I cried. I fought for control. Eventually, I managed to stop crying and broke away from their clutches.

I felt I'd become the focus of the workshop. The practical experiment that made for its success. I cursed the guys from Cork who'd persuaded me to attend the workshop. These guys – one of them was a former lover – didn't have the balls to say they were sorry when Paul died. They'd now taken it upon themselves to decide what was good for me. I was angry. There was no escaping the fact Paul had died from AIDS. My problem remained how to deal with this now-felt-fact.

Chapter Nine

I'm very pleased with your teaching, the principal at the Cobh school told me one day.

She was a nun. She liked to be called by her first name, Ann. That summer she and I were due to take a group of the pupils on an exchange to Ploermel, Cobh's twinned town in Brittany.

There'll be a job coming up for a Business Studies teacher here next year and it's yours, she said.

I was delighted. I couldn't believe my luck. I was a good teacher. With an honours qualification, I still couldn't believe my luck.

Come and talk to me about it next week, she added.

The following week I went to her office.

Come in, she said when I'd knocked on the door. What can I do for you, Ger?

Well, I came to talk to you about the job, I said.

What job?

I looked at her. You told me last week that there'd be a job for me here next year. And you were giving it to me, I said.

She laughed. No Ger, I never said that. You must be mistaken?

I looked at her. You're telling me that you never told me about a job here next year and that you'd give it to me?

I couldn't have told you that, Ger, how would I know what jobs will be available next year?

She was the principal. Principals were expected to know what staff they needed. And it was May after all. We sat in silence. Staring at each other.

I wanted the ground to open up and swallow me. What the fuck was she playing at? Like I'd walk into a principal's office and tell her she'd offered me a job, if she hadn't.

I shook my head. Stood up and walked to the door. I turned towards her.

Ann, you told me last week you were offering me a job here next year. That much I know. I don't know what's happened since then. But I do know that I didn't conjure the job offer out of thin air, I said.

And left the office. Angry and humiliated.

A job vacancy for my subjects in a county Cork school was advertised later that Summer in the education classifieds section of the *Cork Examiner*. The reply was to be sent to a box number. That's always a sign that it's for a religious school. It was in fact for the Cobh school. I applied. I didn't get a reply. My application was never included in those shortlisted.

He isn't suitable, Ann said when asked by a lay colleague in authority why I wasn't considered for the job.

I learned later, from a reliable source, that the gym teacher in the school had been told by a man, a painter, in my swimming club that I was gay. He in turn told Ann and that's why the job offer disappeared. Because I was gay. Nuns are the biggest liars I've met.

What pissed me off most was the double standard of the self-appointed custodian of morality. He was married. Yet he flaunted his extramarital affairs before members of the swimming club when he was away at competitions in other cities.

* * *

I taught in Scoil Stiofain Naofa, a Cork suburban school, for the 1986 academic year. The students were *rough diamonds*. My job was to put a bit of polish on them. And keep them under control. A couple of my first year students had torched their primary school during the summer holidays. They entered secondary school as wards of court. For some the school was the second last stop before prison. The job was taxing. Little progress was made in terms of covering the curriculum.The teaching staff were friendly and supportive. They were real. It was the best school I ever taught in. The staff-room was unpretentious. A rare thing in staff-rooms. It was unfortunate I had the rowdiest first year class.

One day I entered the classroom and discovered two kids wearing balaclavas.They stood on top of their desks and sniffed glue from brown paper bags. I knew that I was right when I decided to teach for only five years. I was just biding my time.

* * *

I'd been celibate since the Winter of 1985. I'd withdrawn into myself and spent too much time thinking about when I'd become ill. I felt it was inevitable. How could this have happened to me? Paul and I'd been sexually active up to May 1983. Safer sex was then unknown in Ireland. I was always depressed.

I cycled to school each day. There was ice on the road

124

one morning. I fell off the bike and cut my knee. I found it difficult to cycle for a few days. Not because of my knee, but because my energy levels were low. I grew tired quickly and perspired a lot. It was like cycling uphill even on the flat. I thought this must be the beginning of the end. And of course I *would* have my night sweats during the day! It was harrowing but I put it to the back of my mind.

You're an idiot, I thought a week later when I discovered the bike's frame had been strained in the fall. The wheel was touching the frame – that's what made the cycling difficult. Not failing health. I obsessed about my health. I felt like a time bomb. I flossed my teeth one morning and noticed a dark red mark on the inside of my cheek. This must be it, I thought. But it was another false alarm. The mark was a bruise. I'd bitten my cheek by accident.

I had many friends. I wasn't lonely. Yet I confided in no one. The biggest problem was the feeling of aloneness. Paul had died. If he loved me, he'd have stuck around. He'd told me two days before he died that I wasn't strong enough to pull him through. So I was abandoned; incapable of being loved. I felt sorry for myself. Things didn't make sense. My life was becoming more and more complicated. My choice of a profession didn't help. An out gay teacher was not part of society's blueprint. But I'd never gone for the easy option.

★ ★ ★

Nobody would have known that I was in turmoil. I was worried my parents would be distraught when they heard I was about to die, as I was sure they would. It was a numbers game. When would my time be up? There were some programmes on television about AIDS. I watched them on the red portable television set in my bedroom. Frightening.

At this stage a test existed to detect antibodies to the virus. I began to think about taking the test. But didn't. I needed time to work out how I'd tell my family. It was as if I had two lives. One ordinary; keeping down a job that paid the rent. The other isolated; living in fear in my head.

Paul felt it unfair that he was dying. Because he'd had such a short innings. It seemed nonsensical to me that I'd die because of love.

I decided to leave Cork three years after I came back to it. I'd found the shelter I was looking for. Temporarily. I moved back to Dublin. I went to my parents for lunch the Sunday I was leaving. I had a blue Mini; my first car. I'd packed my belongings into the car. After lunch Dad directed me out on the terrace and wished me luck.

Your mother and I are sad to see you go. We hoped you'd settle in Cork. I hope we haven't failed you in any way, he said.

I've got to get away. Mum and you've been great. I can't live in Cork anymore, I said.

We looked at each other. Intensely. We were both crying. My father has beautiful sky-blue eyes.

* * *

I was to stay with Joan Sheehy in her flat in Crampton Buildings. Temple Bar hadn't yet become Dublin's hotch-potch version of Covent Garden. I didn't have a job in Dublin. But my luck was in. I was offered a job a week after I arrived in Dublin. My mother called to tell me the good news on Thursday. The bad news was the job was in Limerick.

I think the nun who called is either living in the Middle Ages or desperate to fill the job, she said laughing.

Why's that?

Well, she said, your wages would be very good and you'd be able to save because digs aren't expensive in Limerick.

We both laughed at the thought of what I was letting myself in for. The nun felt certain that I was suitable for the job when I spoke to her the next day.

Could you meet me in Cork on Saturday morning?

Yes, I replied.

We arranged to meet in the Orangery of Cork's Imperial Hotel on South Mall at eleven am. I travelled to Cork with a friend on the Friday evening. I went to the hotel after swimming training on the Saturday morning. I saw her sitting at the low table in the centre of the restaurant. I walked towards her.

Hello, Sister Lelia, I'm Ger Philpott, I said offering my hand.

How did you know it was me?

How do you tell a nun in a nice way you can spot them from fifty paces – without blowing a job interview in the process?

A lucky guess, I said.

She smiled. We ordered morning coffee. She was from Cork. She had grown up in the Lough, on the south-side of the city. And spoke with the proverbial lilting voice. Too nice for words.

Most of the girls you'll be teaching have problem backgrounds, she said.

Great, I thought. Why do I always get to teach the difficult pupils?

Your CV is impressive and you're even better in person. The girls will be mad about you, she said as we shook hands on the deal. I don't expect you to make much progress academically with them but I feel it's important that they'll get to see the good side of masculinity. They're badly in need of a positive male role model.

I was to start work the following Monday morning. We said goodbye. Cheapskate, I thought. She left me to pick up the tab.

So I moved to the southwest. I stayed in a bed-and-breakfast the first evening. I was eaten alive by bedbugs. An auspicious start to life in stab city. I got a basement flat in Perry Square. The job was a job. Nothing more. I couldn't believe I was living in Limerick. But it was as good a place as any to be confused. I guess. I joined a gym and worked out four times a week. It was a strange time. I made good friends in Limerick. A husband and wife and John, a gay man. And two friends from Dublin, who taught part-time in the art college, stayed with me two nights each week. They were my salvation. We went to art exhibition openings. We got drunk. We went to the movies. No matter what was showing. What else do you do in Limerick? I kept on swimming. Limerick's a great place to be depressed!

The school staffroom, with the exception of a few good skins, was a disaster. The place was full of middle-class women dressed in garish Richard Alanesque finery. Their job was to set an example for some of Limerick's most disadvantaged young women. Is it any wonder that many of these students were frustrated? Yes, in many cases school was a reprieve for them from all sorts of abuses. But how unfair that the only expectations given them were way beyond their reach.

* * *

I went to Cork for Christmas and visited friends in Dublin for New Year. I decided the time had come to take an HIV test. I went to Derek Freedman, a well-known sexually-transmitted disease (STD) doctor. When I told him I was Paul's partner he looked up. Surprised. Paul's mother had switched him from being a patient of Dermot Roche to Derek Freedman.

I was only involved at the end. I didn't know Paul had a partner. Nobody told me. If I'd known I'd have asked to see you at the time, he told me.

I thought it strange he hadn't asked if Paul had a partner. Okay, Paul was ill. But, that doesn't make you partnerless. He took a blood sample for testing.

I live in Limerick, it won't be convenient to call back next week, I said. Can I telephone you for the results?

He gave me a code and agreed to give me the results over the phone.

I rang the following Friday morning. I went to a call box in O'Connell Street during a free period at school.

Hello. I'd like to speak to Doctor Freedman, it's Ger Philpott. I'm calling for the results of my HIV test, I said.

What is your code number?

I gave him the code number and he went off.

How are you feeling? he asked when he returned after what seemed an eternity. My stomach churned. My heart sank. I couldn't believe this was happening to me. In a phone booth in Limerick's O'Connell Street!

How should I be feeling, doctor?

Your test results are negative, he said.

You mean I don't have it?

That's correct, he said.

Why did you ask me how I was feeling? You made it sound like I shouldn't be feeling well. And put the heart sideways in me.

I was making conversation.

There're better ways to do that, doctor . . . Thank you, doctor, I said and hung up.

This is incredible. I'm HIV negative. How can this be? I told myself that it didn't matter. It was seconds after I'd received the results. What a difference a few moments can make. I began to cry.

A deep sobbing came from somewhere deep inside me. I'm not going to die. I'm not going to die. I kept repeating to myself as I made my way towards the convent that featured in Kate O'Brien's *Presentation Parlour*. I went back to the pay-phone and called the one friend I'd told about taking the test. The phone wasn't answered. I remembered she was in London showing work at an art exhibition.

There was no one to share my news with. Alone again. Here I was, suddenly, with a future. One I didn't believe existed ten minutes ago. I was reminded of a friend who said, jokingly, when he was diagnosed HIV positive, that he'd never get the bus pass.

I'd grow old. And see my nephews and nieces grow up. It was January 1988. Paul was vivid in my mind's eye. But he'd been dead for almost five years. My heart ached. It had been comforting to think I'd join him. That was now no longer an option. Would I ever love again? I wondered.

Meanwhile I had to get on with my life; and right now that meant going back to school for my next class. Business organisation for a third-year class of rust tartan clad girls in Limerick's Presentation Convent. They liked to call themselves the Dame Studs.

What's wrong with your eyes, asked teachers in the staffroom.

Well actually I've just discovered I won't be having AIDS after all, I thought about saying while I lied about getting dust in my eyes.

I doubt if I underestimated my colleagues in my efforts to protect them from the best news I could've heard. It was lunch-time when my class finished. It was a strain making it to the end of the day.

I went to Roches Stores to do the shopping at the end of the day. I wandered up and down the aisles. Carefully considering each purchase. It reminded me of what a friend said. She compared the wives of some of the city's leading commercial lights to Stepford Wives when she saw them wondering around the shopping centre in Dooradoyle. Lost in some half world. I never thought I'd be grateful for Roches Stores. But I was. I splashed out on champagne. It's such a waste drinking champagne alone. I phoned my sister Joan on the way home. She wasn't there. I wanted to share my good news with someone. Anyone. But there was no one. There were a few people around Limerick who'd have made the right noises – but that wasn't what I needed.

I realised no one knew that I was terrified of developing AIDS, and dying. It would be pointless telling someone my good news. The sheer relief about being HIV negative was mine. And mine alone. No matter what happens in life. Whatever circumstances, I'd learned I was on my own. I hated this lesson. In some ways this was more difficult than Paul's death.

I unpacked the shopping and put the immersion on when I got home. I soaked in a bath till my skin went white and wrinkled; topping up the hot water from time to time. Dinner was strange. Toasting myself and having imaginary conversations as I watched silent movies in my head. My tears were of sadness and joy. I bawled my eyes out. I wanted someone to hold me. Instead I got drunk and listened to Maria Callas arias. Yes, I wallowed in self-pity. I deserved to.

The Munster sprints swimming competition was held in Limerick the following day. I competed in the senior events. As I sat at the side of the pool I was struck by the fact I'd been in a swimming-pool each time my life was affected by AIDS-related events. First Paul's death and now my HIV test results. I haven't yet worked out the significance of this. It wasn't a coincidence.

* * *

I'll never meet anyone in Limerick, went my refrain to John, my gay friend in Limerick. There's nobody in this town for me.

What do you mean?

Well I've been here six months and there hasn't been a whiff of interest from anyone.

There *is* someone who is interested in you, he said.

Who?

I don't know if I should tell you. I don't think you'd be good for each other.

You can't stand there, see me this desperate. And tell me there's someone interested in me and then say it wouldn't be any good. I'll be the judge of that, I said.

Nothing like a bit of intrigue to whet the appetite. John was reticent because my secret admirer was married. And charming.

Can I give you a lift home? he asked when I left my gym the following rainy Monday evening.

I looked up and realised this was my admirer. No longer secret.

I live around the corner, I said.

I know. It's no problem, it'll save you from getting wet, he said unlocking his car doors with the automatic device on his key-ring.

How long have you been a member of the gym? I asked as we turned on to O'Connell Street. I remembered I'd met him at a gathering my first week in Limerick. I'd admired his shoes.

Do you like living in Limerick?

No, I answered.

I don't blame you, he agreed.

We pulled up in front of my flat.

Thank you for the lift, I said as I picked up my bag and opened the door.

Stay a while. Let's talk?

I closed the door. We looked at each other.

This isn't a good idea. This won't be a quick fuck, I said.

I know, he said. We sat in silence for a few minutes.

I've never been involved with a married man. I don't think now is a good time to start.

Why?

None of your business really.

Will you meet me on Saturday? To talk about it?

Adrenalin was pumping through my body.

Where?

At my house.

I looked at him. What about your wife?

She's away.

And your children?

They'll be asleep.

I don't know. Thanks for the lift, I said and got out of the car.

John called the next day.

I hear you got a lift home from the gym last night?

John, this guy is crazy. He's also intriguing, I said.

★ ★ ★

Let's drive up into the Clare Glens and visit Glenstal today, John asked making coffee in my flat the following Saturday morning.

I had a quick shower and we set off.

You're so spontaneous, John, I said as we drove past Annacotty.

We both laughed.

What do you mean?

I've been asking you to go on this jaunt for weeks and you breeze into my flat today and suggest it as if it fell out of the sky?

Hmm, he said.

We'd an enjoyable day walking the hills. The drive into Glenstal Abbey was amazing.

So this is where Paul went to school. We knocked at the door and asked to see Paul's school-friend who I'd met at his funeral. He was now a housemaster there. John and I joked about stealing a photo of a mutual acquaintance who had once been a novice at the abbey from the photo album in the drawing-room while we waited. I stopped John from taking the picture. Against my better judgement.

Paul's friend arrived and gave us a tour of the school. It was strange. And wonderful. Paul had told me many stories about his schooldays. He'd been the head boy at Glenstal. We saw the icon museum.

It'll be wall-to-wall Rolls Royces for miles, the house master joked about the official opening day.

Vespers were the highlight of the visit.

Will you see your fancy-man this evening? John asked laughingly as we drove back to Limerick in the rain.

I don't think so, John. I'm beyond being a bit on the side. Besides I don't know where he lives, I said.

Talking to him won't hurt. I'll give you directions, he said.

You must be mad, I thought to myself as I drove into his driveway later that evening.

I will sleep with you, I agreed. But not in your house. And certainly not with your children asleep upstairs. We had our first tryst the following afternoon. We always met in my flat, unless we were out of town.

We sat on armchairs opposite each other in my living-room. It was mid-afternoon, one day, several months after the affair had begun. We'd just made love. He was facing the windows and I him. We were discussing my planned move to Dublin in a few months.

Pull down the blinds. Quickly, he demanded as he dashed to the wall between the windows and dropped to the floor.

What are you doing? I asked as I pulled the blinds down.

One of your neighbours has walked into the garden, he explained.

He didn't want to be seen. Detected.

How do you think this makes me feel?

The tears rolled down my cheeks. You fool, I thought. You actually believed you'd take on middle-class heterosexual Limerick society and win. I was only a bit on the side . . . I look back at this time now and I realise that, though I was desperate for love and affection, the affair was a big mistake. A valuable lesson. I was trying to replace Paul with an equally deceptive bastard. I also learned that stability is something that comes from within, not without.

* * *

I moved to Dublin when my teaching job ended. I made a pact with myself. To take time out. No more flings or affairs. I'd date people instead and begin to work on the grief I'd locked inside. I was scared at this prospect and tried to think of some way of coping with it. I remember Sunday mornings in the flat in Cork. Soaking in the bath and fantasising about the luxury of being able to afford therapy. I still couldn't afford it. But I'd read in a magazine about the benefits of acupuncture. I could afford a few sessions with an acupuncturist. So, I made some enquiries and an appointment. I'd give it a try.

Chapter Ten

You've been through a traumatic experience, she said knowingly.

I was lying on a couch in an over-warm room overlooking the sea. She laid one of her hands on my chest. She put the other one on my forehead. If she can tell this from a laying-on of hands, she must be pretty good I thought.

Your energy levels are blocked and need to be realigned . . .

My partner died four years ago. He had AIDS, I said.

She looked into my eyes. It was difficult to accept her gaze. I felt she knew what I was thinking.

Have you ever worked with crystals?

Christ, she's a space cadet, I thought.

No, I haven't, I said.

I propose to get rid of the bad energy trapped inside your body and open up the flow of positive energies, she counselled.

This is an amethyst crystal. She showed it to me. It has powerful healing properties. I'll lay this on your forehead and leave you here quietly to let your body get on with the work. Is that all right?

I nodded.

Hold this crystal to your chest, she said placing my hand on a crystal over my sternum. I think it may have been topaz. Close your eyes, she said soothingly.

She left the room.

You've got more money than sense, would've been my parents' reaction. What's going on? The perspiration poured out of me. Talk about being hot and bothered! I was burning like a furnace. I could feel space between my clothes and skin. Clammy space. And a tightening in my throat. Thoughts of *The Exorcist* and *Omen* ran through my mind. But I felt calm once the surge of hot flushes had subsided. I'd no concept of time. I dosed snugly. Warmed in a state of semi-consciousness. I didn't want it to end.

How are you feeling? she asked. She stood by my side.

I hadn't heard her come back into the room.

I feel strange. Disconcerted. Yet, calm, I answered. What's going on, I was on fire?

You've had a lot of negative energy buried deep inside. It needed to be released, she explained. That hasn't been helping you. Now we can re-align the positive energies. They'll work for you in a beneficial way. What do you like to do in your spare time? she asked when I sat up.

How do you mean?

Do you like to read or listen to music?

I do a lot of both, I answered. Why? Is that important, I asked.

I'm going to give you an exercise that will help you with grief work. Practice it in a quiet place for the next week and then come back to see me.

I was to breathe deeply and make a resonant humming sound when I exhaled. This was to help me expel remaining negative energy. I practised it a few times with her and then made an appointment for the following week.

It rained as I ran to the carpark in front of her house.

The waves lashed against the sea-wall. I could just about make out Howth through the mist. I sat in the car and cried. I felt at sixes and sevens. Happy. Sad. Relieved. I'd made a quantum leap about something, though I didn't quite know what. I'd rounded a corner. I turned the key in the ignition of the borrowed car and drove off.

I knew instinctively where I was going. I'd beaten the rush hour traffic. The toll bridge is like a metaphor for the journey I was making, I thought. Crossing from denial to acceptance of grief. I pulled into the parking area outside St Fintan's cemetery. Dusk was gathering. I walked through the lower field up to the higher field. He was buried in the family plot in a corner of the graveyard.

I touched the stone that bore his name along with his father's who'd been buried at sea. Part of me resented what I was doing. I still couldn't make sense of why it happened. Why I'd been set apart by this experience. I wondered if the stone had now destroyed the purple Spring flowers, Remembrance crocuses, I'd planted on his grave a few years before.The tears crept upon me. Slowly.

I'd had enough of crying. I didn't want to shed any more tears. A loud noise came from deep inside me. Suddenly. It was as if something had taken control of me. I wanted to run from the place. But I couldn't. I huddled myself against the spasm and waited for it to subside. It was dark when I climbed back into the car. Something important has happened, I told myself as I drove back to the city.

I'd found out about her from friends. She'd studied oriental medicines in Singapore. I sat in her room and explained the graveyard story to her during my second appointment the following week.

I thought you might go there, she said. Continue with

the exercise I gave you last week. Today, I'll give you some acupuncture to boost your immune system. A tonic. A type of pick-me-up, she said; sticking the needle in to the pad of flesh between my clenched thumb and index finger. I felt high afterwards. The feeling of elation lasted for days.

* * *

I rushed from the shower, dripping a trail of wet footprints behind me.

Hello?

How did last night go? asked my friend Viv.

It was fine. The movie was good fun and dinner went smoothly enough. But it got a bit awkward when I planted a goodnight kiss on his cheek and got out of the car.

What do you mean?

Well, he obviously thought something was going to happen. And it didn't.

He rang me this morning.

What did he say? I asked.

He can't make you out. He said this was the third time you'd gone out. You get on really well but you won't allow things progress. He thinks you're a prick-tease.

Fuck him! I said.

That's the point. He wishes you would.

I thought about when I'd first met Viv. It was at a sports event when we were still at school. Neither of us knew about the other being gay. He's one of my few gay friends that go back that far.

What are you up to anyway? he asked.

I don't feel like sleeping with anyone right now. I told you I was changing the patterns of my life. I've messed myself up over the last number of years going out with a shower of wankers. I don't want to do that anymore. I'm enjoying dating people. Getting to know someone without sex getting in the way. It's like having a gay adolescence. Imagine how different we'd be if we'd dated other guys when we were teenagers. Instead of being uptight. And guilt-ridden.

Your new-found-old-fashioned-boy stuff is certainly generating intrigue, Viv laughed.

Well the funny thing about it is that they're all much more attentive, I answered.

We should have thought of this years ago, we agreed; laughing.

Gossip aside, there's a substitute job going in King's Hos. The Business Studies teacher is going on pregnancy leave. Are you interested? he asked.

Protestant, boarding school, thick, rich and creamy kids. At least there's a swimming-pool, I thought.

Sure, I said. When does it start?

It'll be for three months, starting in two weeks time and you'd have to live in. I know the teacher, and if you're interested, it'll be a formality. You'll have to talk to the headmaster.

Yeah, I'm interested.

Lots of gay people have gone through King's Hos, I thought. It wouldn't be the worse place in the world to teach.

The meeting with the headmaster and the Business Department head teacher went well.

Do you mind if I speak to one of your referees? asked the headmaster.

No. Not at all. The principal in Pres convent said she'll be happy to give me a reference.

It's just a formality, he added.

He gave me the timetable and all arrangements were in place. Can you call next Thursday morning, Ger? I'll give you starting time then, he said.

Sure. What time, about eleven?

That'll be fine, he answered.

* * *

Hello, Mr Philpott, he said.

Odd, I thought. Not Ger this time.

I've called to find out what time you wish me to start next week?

I'm afraid we have a slight problem, Mr Philpott.

What's the problem?

We don't think you'll be up to teaching honours accounting, he said.

I don't understand. Last week both you and the Business Department head considered me suitable for the job when you interviewed me. Why have you changed your minds?

We just feel that you wouldn't be able to do the best job.

That's rubbish. Of course I'm up to the job. And you know it.

Mr Philpott, I spoke to the principal of the Limerick school and now feel that you're not suitable for the post. You told me the principal of the Limerick school was willing to act as a referee on your behalf.

I'd be delighted to put in a good word for you, Ger. Sher you're one of our own, the nun had said in her Cork drawl; smiling from behind her desk when I asked her to be my referee.

You shouldn't have given me her name when she wasn't prepared to recommend you for this job.

What do you mean this job?

As you're aware the job involves residential duties.

So?

Under the circumstances it wouldn't be appropriate for you to be given the position. I don't understand.

You know what I'm referring to, Mr Philpott.

No I don't.

Look, Mr Philpott, as you can imagine we're very busy at present with term just started.

I don't care how busy you are. You gave me the job. And my timetable. It's outrageous that you think you can treat me this way. How dare you? I want you to tell me exactly why you've changed your mind?

Mr Philpott, I've got no intention of explaining why I consider you unsuitable for the job. You know I'm not going to do that. You know very well what I mean.

Because I'm gay, is that it?

Mr Philpott, I don't think there's any point continuing this conversation.

And I think you're a hypocrite, sir.

* * *

I picked up a pizza and bought an expensive bottle of wine, later that evening. I parked the car outside the friend's cottage I was caretaking near the Five Lamps on Dublin's northside. I watched the TV as I ate and drank. The phone rang.

What are you doing? the voice on the other end asked.

Oh! I'm here licking my wounds. Feeling sorry for myself.

143

What's wrong? Viv asked

Well your job in King's Hos isn't going to materialise after all.

Why not?

Because I'm queer!

What! Get out of it?

I'm already half way through a great Australian Cabernet, I sighed.

Are you serious about the job?

Yep. I called today to find out when I was due to start next week and he said I wasn't suitable. That it wouldn't be appropriate for me to do the job because it involved residential duties. Apparently the bitch in Limerick knows I'm gay and passed the good news on to yer man and bingo, I'm out of a job.

Ger I'm sorry, Viv said. I'm afraid I've got more bad news, he added as I lay down on the bed. Pour yourself another glass of wine.

I complied. What's the news?

Barry's dead . . .

Shit! When?

This evening.

Fuck it, I thought I'd problems. He was such a lovely man. As if that made it worse.

We went shopping for gaudy ties the last time I saw him, I told Viv. We giggled at Barry's taste in loud ties. We'd lunch in Giordani's with another friend who was also HIV positive . . .

Are you okay? he asked.

Yes. No.

Do you want me to come around?

No, I don't think so. I'm better off on my own, I said and hung up.

The scale of the problem hadn't yet sunk in for most people. In Ireland. When is this going to end?

* * *

You're not camp and you're not butch, Barry said to me one night as we danced in the Hirschfeld – a gay club.

What does that make me?

Interesting. So use it, he added smiling. He had an infectious smile. He was doing a thesis on Lawrence and had gone out with my friend Sean. The guy who'd driven me to Dublin to spend my first weekend with Paul. A life-time ago.

* * *

I felt the softness of my alpaca jumper and breathed the blackcurrant nose of the wine. And savoured its velvety softness on my tongue. Absence of sensation. That's what it's like to be dead. No fucking sensations.

* * *

The crowd gathered outside the crematorium in Glasnevin. I didn't know if I could keep this together. I'd lost lots of friends at this stage. They'd all lived abroad. This was the first back, in Ireland. Since Paul. The time lag was catching up. Sean stepped out of his car and we hugged.

How're you doing, I asked. We looked at each other through tear-filled eyes.

It's nice to see you, he said as we cried. I wish it was under better circumstances, he added. You know Ger, I really loved him. This isn't fair. Not for Barry.

* * *

Inside, the small crematorium was packed. I couldn't help smile when I heard *Each morning I wake up, before I put on my make-up* . . . on the PA system. That's Barry for you. He went out bringing a smile to everyone's faces. His was the first self-planned service I was at. There've been too many since then. And they're not over. Yet.

* * *

I reneged on my commitment to dates and no sex. I met someone different.

The sun shone through the baywindow, across the table, of my Leeson Park flat. We sat clad in our white robes. Sunday newspaper supplements scattered on the floor. Johnny Hartman's *They say that falling in love is wonderful* . . . played on the stereo.

They're looking for teachers in the Bahamas, he said over his newspaper.

Let's apply, I answered from behind my newspaper.

Would you go?

Would you go?

We smiled . . . I came back from work and found the official, crested orange, letter in my hallway. The interviews were held at the Bahamian Embassy in London on St Patrick's Day. We both got jobs and headed off with our two-year contracts under our arms. We spent a week in New York en route.

Our luck was in. We were both posted to Grand Bahama Island. We rented a flat in a luxury block on the beach in an exclusive part of the island. Turquoise sea visible through the glass-fronted building. The beach stretched for miles. The light was iridescent. But for a handful of neighbours, it was private. We bought a car and a wind-surfer. I swam for miles every day. You could swim out beyond the reef and spear fresh lobster. A world apart. And it appeared idyllic. But it wasn't.

We never set up the second bedroom. It was used occasionally for visitors and as a laundry-room for drying clothes. The sun bleached the colour out of most things. So we dried them indoors.

The flat was littered with drying clothes that Saturday evening. We spent the day catching up on laundry and chores. I was half-awake-half-asleep. I noticed movement at the end of the bed. It was hard to make out what it was in the dark. There was someone in the flat! It was a man. A black man. I waited for a moment and nudged John, my partner, awake.

What's wrong?

I think there's someone in the flat, I said.

Stop-talkin! The voice came from outside the open bedroom door. Don-move, he commanded, as we tried to sit up. Lie don.

What the fuck's going to happen to us, I thought.

I tensed my body; drawing my wits about me. I saw that the sliding glass doors to the balcony were ajar. That's how he got in. But I remembered closing them. I could roll out of bed and make a dash for it. But what about my rigid partner lying terrified next to me? I wondered if we were thinking the same thing?

Tell-me-wher-de-money-is? He laughed. He sounded high. Or drunk. Possibly both. He'd now entered the room and had his head covered, shawl-like, with a towel. Okay-you-boyse-do-as-I-say-an-notin-gonna-happin, he sniggered.

There'd been a spate of robberies, recently, in which men were raped in preference to women. These guys would get up on a gust of wind. This is certainly not how I'd envisaged my first sex with a black man.

You-boyse-DEA [Drug Enforcement Agency]?

The US Drug Enforcement Agency were posted to the Bahamas in an attempt to curb drug-smuggling.

Com-now-mon-tell-me-where-de-guns-are.

Neither of us answered. I thought about saying yes. But felt it would be unwise.

How-com-you-white-boyse-are-in-de-bed-together? You-sissy-mon?. No-wearin-no-jocks. I-see-dem-on-de-floor. Which-wan-de-pussy? I-got-sumtin-big'n'black-fer-de-white-boyse. Hee! Hee! Hee!

There's some money in the dresser drawer next to me, I said. I knew then that John was locked in fear and there was no way that we could make a run for it. I was terrified. But I also knew I'd have to keep it together. To think rationally, otherwise all was lost. I still couldn't make out for certain if he was alone. He pulled the drawer of the wicker dresser open. I realised that there were only about seventeen dollars there. Shit! He'd think I was fucking him around.

Hey-mon-der's-no-much-money-her?

Look that's all I've got. You can take my cheque book too. Just take it and go.

He laughed.

Dais-wan-her-mus-be-de-pussy, he said slapping John's leg.

Hadn't he ever heard of versatility?

John was silent. But for his loud breathing. He kept his US currency in a drawer in the living-room. He'd counted about four hundred dollars that day. We were due to go to

Haiti in a few weeks.

Why didn't he tell this guy about the four hundred dollars? The machete flashed, catching the light from outside. Shit! He sensed I noticed this.

I-hav-gun-too-mon, hee! hee! he said, and held it up to show me.

Is it really a gun? He put the gun to John's mouth
I-don-wanna-hert-you-boyse.

I freaked. There's a tall dresser in the living-room. Near the kitchen.There's about four hundred dollars in the second drawer from the top.

You-boyse-stay-wher-you-are. Don-do-notin-foolish!.

I heard him open the drawer. I jumped from the bed. Naked and vulnerable. And reached into the hallway for the doorknob. The door opened out from the bedroom. His hand grabbed the door from the other side just as I'd almost closed it. He yanked it out of my hand. And pushed me back on the bed. He was laughing all the time. I sat back up and roared for help at the top of my voice.

Der-ain-no-one-gonna-her-you, he laughed. Now-lie-down. I-gonna-teech-you-a-lesson. He lifted his hand. I saw the machete coming down towards me.

This is it, I thought. Memories of my childhood fast-forwarded through my mind. I could see my friends Annette and Kay. I was safe then. I've never told my parents that I'd loved them. At least not since I'd grown up. Shit, am I going to die? . . . I felt it hit above my right knee. And then it poked me hard in the groin. I was steeled against the blow. Meanwhile he continued to laugh. And my partner was paralysed beside me.

I waited. My body was numbed. Am I cut? What damage is done? If I can wriggle my toe then it can't be too serious. *The knee bone connected to the thigh bone . . .*

The balcony door was still open. If I can walk then I'm going to make a run for it. On my own. The thoughts dashed through my head. Yes, I can move my toes. Relief. I moved my hand slowly towards my thigh. I couldn't feel any moisture. No blood. I figured he must have used the flat side of the blade. He's not going to kill us. Not yet. What about rape? Who'll be first? I won't be raped. No matter what. When would this be over?

Don-you-pul-sumtin-like-dat-again, he said. Pu-de-pillow-over-yer-heds-mon-an-pu-yer-hans-on-de-top. Now! he shouted. Do-it! he ordered.

Do as he says, I encouraged John. I now realised he was trance-like.

I could hear him in the other room and then silence. Laughter. He was back in the bedroom.

Goode-boyse, he said.

This pattern continued. He's building up the period of silence. Testing us. To give himself enough time to get the money, I thought. He turned out the contents of the drawer on the bed.

Hee! Hee! I-knowd-you-white-boyse-hav-de-monies. Hey-mon, he said hitting my leg. Get-yerself-sum-reel-pussy-mon. I-like-you. Yous-a-fighter-mon. Don-be-messin-roun-wi-de-boys. Dats-okay-for-de-lock-up! Lots-a-bitches-wan-de-white-dick-mon. Dey-wan-de-light-skin-baby. Now-Ise-gonna-hav-a-drink-mons. You-boyse-hav-nuff-boose-out-der-fer-a-party. Hee! Hee! Weese-goona-hav-a-reel-gud-time. Hee! Hee! Hee! Don-u-boyse-do-notin-stupid. Ye-her. Hee! Hee!

Again the pattern of silence and laughter continued. I was scared that if he was drinking then rape was inevitable . . . Why was John not doing anything? I nudged him. No response.

I'm going to close the door, I whispered. You're to drop off the balcony and raise the alarm. Move quickly when I give you the go-ahead. Okay?

I just can't lie here, I thought. I counted silently to ten and dashed for the door. I pulled it shut. This time no one pulled it open. I turned the clasp. And held the handle tight. What if he shoots through the wall? I thought . . .

Get out of bed and get help, I whispered to my partner. No response. Get up and do as I say, I shouted.

No, what if he's still there. He'll kill us, he said.

I'm not going to wait for that. Now get up and get moving! John dropped off the balcony and ran towards the caretaker's office. I looked into the living-room from the balcony. He was gone. Relief. Yet terror. What if he was in the bush waiting?

The caretaker's called the police, he said. Are you okay? he asked embracing me when he returned.

Don't. We've got to get things together.

What do you mean?

You know how homophobic the cops are here? We've got to protect ourselves. We'd better make up the second bedroom and work out a story about what happened. If these guys know we're gay, we're fucked.

We began to fix up the other room. And work out what happened. Who noticed him first? When did he put us into the same room? The whole fucking shebang. I cried with rage. This was adding insult to injury. I also knew that the relationship was over.

* * *

We went on separate holidays that Summer. I left first and went to Central America. He went to Canada. As far apart

151

as possible on the same continent. We met up in San Francisco. Our Swan Song. He decided to go back to Ireland. I'd return to the Bahamas.

Goodbye, I said as he climbed into the Airport limousine. We kissed.

Take care of yourself, he said.

I smiled. When the bus had turned the corner I walked to Cafe Flores on Market Street for breakfast.

* * *

I met Jonathan in a nightclub two weeks later. He was part Cherokee, part Masi. He was magnificent. Dumb, yet magnificent. I returned to the Bahamas but promised to come back the following year.

* * *

The bank holiday was due in a few weeks. Rock fever was setting in. So I planned to go to Miami on a shopping trip. I swapped my Miami ticket for one to San Francisco. I jumped my contract and headed for the west coast of America. Lock. Stock. And Barrel. I reported to school early. Signed the day-book and then drove to the airport. I was sad to leave. Because I'd become good friends with a small number of Bahamians. I liked them. But I was bored with the monotonous beauty of paradise. The sense of relief as the plane climbed into the air was tremendous. My life was about to begin again.

* * *

I can't believe I waited until my thirties to live in San

Francisco. Some people never get there! I can't describe what it was like to live there. All the validation I was robbed of, growing up in hetero-land, was paid back with dividends.

Hello?

I looked at him and returned his smile. This was casual flirtation. No pressure at all. And I'm only going to the dry-cleaners. Jesus, you'd be lucky to get an hello out of someone in a gay bar in Dublin, I thought. Gay people didn't confine their sexuality to after-dark places. Gay people are everywhere in San Francisco. In shops. Restaurants. Dry-cleaners. No big deal. It's not the bars or clubs. Nor is it Castro Street and the gay scene. They're all part of it. It was *The good ship Lolli-pop* . . . Without Shirley Temple!

I was also struck by the visibility of AIDS. Again. It's accepted in this city where one-in-two gay men over twenty-five are HIV positive. But that's not to say that men who are HIV-negative don't carry the burden of the epidemic, too. The guilt. The sense of loss. People care. My life would be good in San Francisco. Good friends. Challenging work where my contribution was appreciated and hundreds of beautiful men. Sexy confident men who smiled at will. But there's more to life.

I realised I was one of those Irish people who goes abroad to find that he really wants to live in Ireland. The down side of San Francisco was that it was in America, California. A place where, beyond the AIDS epidemic, there's a complete denial of death. An artificial society.

I swam with the University of San Francisco Masters and Tsunami, a gay and lesbian swim team. I was ranked top in my age-group and all these hunks were asking me for stroke technique advice. Such interest! Can you help me with my stroke-technique? Can I what! Valhalla!

I drove to the pool for training each weekday morning at 5.30 am. Mary Robinson has been elected President of Ireland, the voice on the radio announced. She defeated Brian Lenihan and Austin Currie. Fan-fucking-tastic! What a sea change. A woman as *Head of State*. I'd met Mary Robinson once, about ten years earlier, to discuss gay law reform with her at a Labour Party conference in Cork. I'd also seen her at a few anti-amendment campaign fund-raisers in Dublin during the Summer of 1983. Her election swung my vote to return. I knew I was going home as I swam up and down the pool.

★ ★ ★

I pushed the trolley through the arrivals gate struggling to keep my six bags on board. It wasn't easy. I'd cracked three ribs on a kamikaze run down a mogul-field skiing in Nevada before my return. The airport bustled with exiles returning for Christmas. Dorothy, my lift, was late. I called my sister Joan. Lift and sister turned up together.

Charming! Great homecoming this is, I teased. Neither of the two had money. I paid for the coffee. Aghh! I roared.

What's wrong, they both asked, startled.

I'm in agony. I cracked three ribs skiing, I answered.

Eejit, my sister said as I stuck my tongue out at her.

They both laughed hysterically. I joined them.

Aghh! Stop. Don't make me laugh. It hurts, I cautioned.

The laughing and screaming continued. We left the coffee bar. Much to the relief of those drinking coffee around us. We'd to walk miles to the carpark.

Typical! I said.

What? they asked.

The busiest time for passenger traffic. Christmas bloody week. And they decide to build a new shagging carpark in the airport. God, it's great to be home, I added throwing my eyes up to the grey sky.

We laughed.

Aghh! Don't, I said clutching my ribs, as we giggled our way to the car.

* * *

I travelled to Cork a few days later. I discovered that the Names Quilt was to stage an Irish tour shortly after Christmas. The idea for the memorial Quilt was conceived in San Francisco. It was an effort to pool grief and to make a visible gesture to the often invisible deaths of those who'd died from AIDS. It was also used as a powerful lobbying tool in the US. I'd worked as a volunteer at the San Francisco Quilt workshop office. Would I make a panel for Paul? I thought about this over Christmas and discussed it with one of my old gay politico-friends.

Come to a meeting in the co-op to discuss the tour, he invited.

Clare was one of the two national tour coordinators. She was impressive. I decided that I'd contribute a panel in memory of Paul.

Good man, Ger! said Clare encouragingly. Do you know anyone who can speak Irish? she asked. We need someone to do an interview with *Cursai*, the Irish language current affairs programme.

I speak Irish, I said.

Will you do the interview?

I'll think about it. Can I call you when I get back to Dublin?

* * *

I walked into Hickeys fabric shop in Patrick Street on Christmas Eve. I didn't know what material to buy. I'd made bean bags to earn money when I was in college. But I was daunted by the fact that I hadn't used a sewing machine for years. The material picked itself. It was a shiny satin, aquamarine coloured. It reminded me of the sea. Jung's collective unconscious.

* * *

My father and eldest brother, Barry, brought me to the train station when I was returning to Dublin. I met an old friend in the queue for the train. The last time I'd seen him, three years ago, we'd spent a weekend in New York's gay Shangri-la, Fire Island.

How are you? It's so good to see you.

And you, he smiled.

We'd met first at a party more than ten years earlier. We hardly noticed the train journey passing as we caught up on the past couple of years. The rain pelted against the window. We drank coffee and ate the standard cardboard-like fruit cake. I can't remember what it was he said. Perhaps it was more the way he said it? But I knew he was HIV-positive. Another Quilt panel to be made, I imagined.

* * *

The Quilt tour was due to start on January 13th. I busied

myself with Paul's panel. I learnt to use Joan Sheehy's sewing-machine. She was giving this homeless soul refuge, not for the first time. I'd a viyella shirt of Paul's. It'd belonged to his grandfather. I cut out the letters from it and spelled his name and the date of his death. I felt it important to add something further. *Change a little and a lot can happen*, he'd written to me once. When I'd been reluctant to go out with him eleven years earlier. That's appropriate, I thought. I'd put this on the border. Around the edges. I persevered with the panel. It was difficult, not so much because of my bad sewing. But because of the feelings it brought up. I became totally wrapped up in the Quilt. I poured my heart into every stitch. I embroidered the past seven years of aloneness into it.

Progress was slow. And the tour was imminent. I admitted defeat after putting on his name and the date of his death. I asked the women volunteers at the Quilt office to sew on the border's message. I nearly died when I called in, one day, to check on things.

You'll have to take it off, I said. They'd used this outrageous camp lurex thread to write the message on the panel. Very un-Paul and non-me. Please use the navy tape I've given you.

We thought this was more colourful, they said.

No. Use the navy.

They did. And I was grateful for their help.

I helped the tour coordinators, Clare and Rachel, with publicity arrangements. I'd agreed to do the *Cursai* interview. It was due to start at four.

I went home to Joan's flat to change. Yes, ten percent of the population is gay and ten per cent of the population speaks Irish. But let's tell the other ninety per cents what I'm on about, I thought as I slipped the T-shirt on. Loring had designed it as part of an Act-Up demonstration in New York.

It showed an old photograph of two sailors, two men kissing. The caption beneath read *Read my Lips*.

I was handed the official Quilt tour T-shirt back in the Quilt office.

Will you put this T-shirt on? It'll be better.

Yes, I'm back in Ireland, I thought. But on my terms. So get used to it. No thanks this one's fine, I answered.

My first overt political act in the fight against AIDS in Ireland. Let the nation squirm. All those who watch *Cursai* at any rate. I was nervous doing the interview. I gave my all to the camera and the very capable Anna Huseuff who interviewed me. When I saw it I was struck by how sad I looked.

My mother was struck by it in another way. So to speak! Both my parents are religious and daily Mass-goers. She walked out under the impressive Corinthian pillars of the portico of the Dominican Saint Mary's on Cork's Pope's Quay, after her daily devotions. So did another woman.

How dare your son wear that disgusting T-shirt on the telly? You should be ashamed of yourself, she said as she pushed my mother against a pillar.

My son can wear whatever he likes on television, my mother replied, startled. How can *you* behave like this in the house of God? she added and walked away.

My mother told me this story later, when I was in Cork to speak at the opening of the Cork leg of the tour. But more about that later.

The *Cursai* interview was well received.

Congrats, said Clare and Rachel. Would you speak next Sunday at the opening ceremony in the Mansion House?

Yes, I'd be happy to do that. Thank you for asking me, I replied.

That Saturday night they showed the Academy Award winning documentary, Common Threads, on the genesis of the Quilt on TV, they also discussed it on the *Late Late Show*.

I walked purposefully up Dawson Street. I wore Paul's narrow leather belt around my waist. With my heart in my mouth. His family had objected to the panel and wanted it removed. Over my dead body! They can't rob me of this expression of my grief.

I walked towards the door of the Mansion House Round Room.

Ger, how are you? Paul's brother Denny asked.

I'm fine. How are you?

Mother is very upset about the panel, he said.

I've discussed this with her, Denny. This is just something I have to do for me.

You're determined to do it?

Yes.

Paul would like it. You've done a great job. I wish someone cared the same way about me. It must've been difficult for you?

It hasn't been easy.

We looked at each other.

I have to go in, I said.

Good-bye, he replied as we hugged.

I met with the tour committee and put my case to them. They decided that the panel would stay. In any event removing it at this late stage would have generated the wrong type of publicity for the family. At one point, Paul's elder brother had threatened to take me to court. It was laughable.

I climbed on the stage to rehearse. I'd no idea what I was going to say. But that'd come later. I noticed him in the corner of the stage. He was crouched on his haunches sorting out the sound system. Dark and ruggedly handsome, I thought.

Hello, he said looking up.

Hi, I replied. His smile was beautiful.

I'm the most-non-technical-technical-helper they could've found. I haven't a clue what I'm doing, he said.

If this guy is straight, it'd be a pure waste, I thought. I walked around the block to calm my nerves. The Mansion House's Round Room was choc-a-bloc. I sat on stage waiting for my turn to speak. My heart pounded. And the perspiration dripped from my armpits like a running tap. What the fuck was I going to say? The speakers before me broke into tears. Don't cry, I told myself. I walked to the micro-phone. And looked through the crowd. There were no words. I'd dried up. The knot in my throat got bigger.

I . . . feel . . . privil . . . eged . . . to . . . be . . . here . . . today . . .

I had to fight to get each word out. It was a nightmare. I beat the tears back. And finished my speech quoting the words on the border of Paul's panel, *Change a little and a lot can happen*. Liam O'Maonlaoi, of Hot House Flowers fame played a heartrending lament on a tin whistle.

Then I broke down. People were invited from the balcony to examine the Quilts. Those on the stage hugged each other. I wanted to run, but stayed.

I think you're very brave, he said hugging me!

I thought I could die in his arms. I couldn't leave. I hung around for a while talking to people. Fighting for control.

Would you like to go for a coffee? I asked him.

Yes, he turned, smiling.

We went to Bewley's and chatted about swimming and therapy. We returned to the Mansion House, then repaired to Keoghs for pints and afterwards to a nearby Pizza restaurant. I explained the story of the difficulties with Paul's family. He put his hand on my leg and rubbed my thigh. Supportive. We agreed to meet the following Wednesday. After the Quilt closing ceremony. Meanwhile, he was going to London on business. We kissed on Dawson Street. I went on to a nightclub to dance and get drunk.

* * *

Hello, I just called to say I'm looking forward to Wednesday evening, he said when I answered the phone.

I've got a mother of a hangover.

Well, if you will indulge, he laughed.

See you Wednesday, I said hanging up.

* * *

We left the closing ceremony. He'd been a pillar of strength during the difficult moments; holding my hand.

I thought we might go to the Runner Bean, he said as we walked into the cold night air.

I felt great. I'd closed a chapter of my life which had hung over me for too long. We kissed in the car. The dinner was romantic. Intimate looks over revelations of life-stories. Playing with food on the plates. Odd to have your first date with someone you'd met, effectively, at your former lover's funeral. Yes, this would be interesting, I thought.

I've got something I want to tell you, he said.

What could it be? Shoot, I said looking into his eyes.

I'm HIV positive.

My innards did triple somersaults. I raised the glass to my mouth and drank some wine. Our gaze didn't break contact.

I don't have a problem with that.

I didn't think you would but I thought it important to tell you before we slept together.

Are we sleeping together this evening? I enthused.

Can it wait until the weekend?

Sure, I said.

We kissed in the car as he dropped me off.

My steps were heavy as I climbed the metal stairs of Crampton Buildings. I fell into bed and turned the TV on. I surfed the channels. The Gulf War broke out this evening, the announcer said. I started to cry. The phone rang.

Hello baby!, Kay said. Why are you crying? Is it because of the Gulf War?

No.

Didn't the date go well?

It was great.

What's the problem, honey?

Kay, he's HIV positive.

Chapter Eleven

I walked along Cork's North Main Street with my mother. She was going to town to shop. And I had a meeting to go to.

The T-shirt you wore on the *Cursai* programme – it had a photo of two men in sailors' outfits, kissing. Was there a particular reason for wearing it? she asked.

Yes. I wanted to make a visual statement about what I was doing, I replied.

Not everyone watching would've understood Irish. So I wasn't leaving anything to chance.

Will you be wearing it again? she wanted to know.

I haven't planned to, I answered as we looked at each other.

We were coming to the crossroad at which we would part company. She to do her shopping and me to do an interview for Cork local radio.

I'm one hundred per cent behind what you're doing, she added. I think you're very brave. You know that. Dad, and I will defend you against any criticism. But, some people will react badly to the T-shirt. You wouldn't want to *over-wear* it, Ger, she said knowingly.

I nodded. We smiled.

I'm heading down this way. Mum gestured with her head as we approached the corner of Castle Street. Will you be home later for tea?

Yes I will, I said. See you about half-five. We kissed and parted.

She's great, I thought as I made my way to the Cork AIDS Alliance offices.

The offices are located in the *Marsh* area of the city. As the name suggests, it's a damp, dank part of the city. The building stands in a dead-end laneway. When I got there I went up to the attic room and waited for Alf McCarthy from RTE. He's a good guy, somebody said as we waited for him.

But he'll probably focus on the gay dimension to the story, someone else said.

He arrived late. I found it strange talking on the hoof about the story.

What was it like telling your parents you were gay? Are they supportive of you? What was it like when your lover was sick?

I realised that I hadn't discussed what I was doing with my parents. Apart from telling them I was making a commemorative panel for Paul. And that I would be speaking at the Quilt opening.

I often wondered about that, my father said when I told him a few days earlier that Paul had died from AIDS.

Are *you* okay? was his next question.

I hadn't thought through whether my parents would agree or disagree with what I was doing. I was glad that my mother had said, shortly before the interview, that they supported me. I realised then that I didn't fully understand the consequences, the repercussions of what I was doing.

I feel incredibly lucky to be healthy, I told Alf McCarthy. I feel I have an obligation, because of this good fortune, to speak publicly about my story.

He was a good guy – as I was told. He made me feel relaxed, at ease. I was a bit shell-shocked afterwards. I went home to rest before the opening ceremony later that night.

* * *

If it hadn't been a solemn occasion, the idea of coming out that night on the stage of Cork's City Hall would have been hilarious. I went through the building's back door. It was Thursday the seventeenth of January 1991. Childhood memories flooded back. The swimming-pool next door. The countless hours I'd spent there training as a competitive swimmer. The weight-training sessions with my swimming club mates in the Corporation yard behind the building. My stint as a life-guard at the pool during school and university holidays. The Corporation meetings I saw from the public gallery when my father was a Labour Councillor during my teenage years. I knew the place like the back of my hand.

City Hall was part of my history. I first climbed on to its stage, as part of my national school's choir, when I was six or seven. We were competing in Cor Fheile na Scoile. I'd also been on the stage as a drunken teenager, dancing, at discos and concerts. But, that January night I climbed on stage for a different reason. To tell people that my lover, Paul, had died from AIDS. I didn't know what I was going to say.

But, it felt right that, whatever I was going to say, I was to say it in Cork.

My childhood had been linked with this building, this part of the city. I swam my first length of the swimming-pool when I was four years of age. It was night-time. And

I felt big and important. I didn't feel at all big or important the night the Quilt opened.

How do you want to be introduced? asked the EmmCee, a local journalist, as I climbed on stage for the tiresome rehearsal. And what are you going to say? she continued.

You can introduce me by name, I said. I don't know what I'm going to say.

Well, how long will it take you to speak?

I don't know. As long as it takes me, I answered.

I was angry as I left the stage. This was a big deal for me. Not a performance. I knew she was only doing her job. But, I felt she was cold. Insensitive.

The hall was beginning to fill up. It was strange to see so many familiar faces. People I knew at school. At university. People my parents knew. People who knew my parents. I was nervous. But, I stood tall in my you-can't-get-me-armour.

* * *

The Quilts were unfolded, flag-like. Four people dressed in white, and without shoes, opened them out, ceremonially, from the centre. They started by lifting each of the four folded corners and placing them on the ground. They continued to lift each of the remaining folded corners out. They moved clock-wise as they carried on. They had to stand on the Quilt as it spread out. When they lifted the last folded corners out they didn't place them on the ground. Instead they stretched the quilt as they walked in a circle. The Quilt was lifted into the air. It was spectacular. It caught the air and floated, in slow-motion, down to the ground. When the would-be pall-

166

bearers checked that each corner was in its designated place, they moved on in single file. To the next Quilt. Sad pensive music played to accompany the ceremony.

★ ★ ★

I waited for my turn to climb on stage. The space at the left-hand side of the stage was reserved for speakers and organisers. It was full of people crying. I steeled myself. I still didn't know what I was going to say.

I climbed on stage and stood behind the microphone. The lighting made it difficult to see the faces in the crowded hall. Good.

My years as a teacher stood me in good stead. I was able to move my gaze around the hall as I spoke.

I remember I climbed up on this stage as a young child with my national school choir at Cor Fheile na Scoile, I said.

How nervous I was then, I thought. And now. I don't remember exactly what I said then. It was about how life takes on a momentum of its own and something about there not being any guarantees.

I told the audience that the young child I was, had been, couldn't know that he'd climb on the stage as an adult to talk about his lover's death.

I dug my hands deep into my pockets and spread my legs for support. I felt numbed as I wondered what words would next come out of my mouth. I finished what I had to say. I climbed down from the stage. And I broke down. Vulnerable. Exposed.

★ ★ ★

The RTE interview was broadcast the next day. It was a miserable wet Friday. My father lent me his car. I went off to Kinsale for the day with the Irish Quilt tour coordinators and the American organiser. We checked in at the exhibition at City Hall before heading off. We listened to the interview on the car radio as the *tor-i-en-chal* rain beat down on the car roof. I tried hard to swallow the lump in my throat as I thought about my parents and my aunt who lived a few doors down the street in Blarney Street.

The radio was always on in our house at lunch-time. I felt for them. For their vulnerability. But there was no turning back now. And this was something I had wanted to do for a long time. It was bizarre. I'd mulled the story over and over again in my head for years. Now I'd talked openly about it. On radio. And in my hometown.

* * *

Mam and I listened to your interview today, my father told me later that evening. Did you hear the interview?

No, I lied.

It was very good, Ger. he said. You were extremely articulate.

Did I sound very well-dressed? I asked jokingly. I referred to a family joke about my father when he did work-related interviews as a Corporation member.

Speaking like that. Publicly. Takes a lot of courage, he said as we avoided each other's eyes. You're very brave, son.

What you're doing is important, both he and my mother said.

I made an excuse about being tired and went to bed.

168

The next day I argued with my aunt about the interview.

Are you sure you know what you're doing? she quizzed me coldly.

What do you mean? I asked. Of course I know what I'm doing. But she wasn't convinced. Then I pulled a mean trick.

I was there for you when Nana died, I said. I have to do this now and get on with my life. And I need your support. Not your antagonism.

I'm just concerned for you, love, she said as she turned toward me.

We looked at each other. We hugged and cried. I knew, when I mentioned my grandmother's death, that she'd rally around.

The three people I'd worried most about upsetting were now on side. Everything is okay now, I thought.

I went to a dinner party that night. A group of Cork gay politicos. I felt good about the past few days. My world had been turned on its head. A burden had been lifted. That is, except for my thoughts about the new *man* in my life. I couldn't put him out of my mind.

Why are you doing this? I kept asking myself. You've just laid the memory of one man who died from AIDS to rest. And now you're dating someone else who's HIV positive. Why?

Would you go out with someone who was HIV positive? I asked the group of men sitting around the table.

What do you mean? one of them replied. And they say Kerrymen only answer a questions with questions!

They all scored full points for the politically correct, yes, answer.

Do you mean would I have sex with someone who is HIV positive? another asked.

No, that's not what I mean, I said as I thought of the sex I'd had with *him* the previous weekend. I let the topic die. As I wondered about the differences between mortality and *proscribed* mortality.

I went back to Dublin the next day. The phone rang as I turned the key in the door on that cold Sunday evening.

Hello, love, my aunt said.

How are you? I said. I'm just in the door.

I won't delay you, she said. I just called to tell you that your mum, dad and I went to see the Quilt before the closing ceremony this evening.

I was dumbstruck.

We really liked Paul's panel.

Thank you, I said.

Your sewing could be better though, she snapped before she hung up.

* * *

It was raining heavily. O'Connell Street was awash. I skirted along the side of buildings for shelter.

Hello, young Philpott, he said as we bumped into each other. It was a colleague of my father's from Cork. His name was Brendan. He was making his way into the Gresham Hotel. I was about to cross to the other side of the road.

God it's a lousy day, he said in his Cork drawl.

Cats and dogs, I replied.

I want to say something to you, boy. You're a man among many.

I remembered that whenever the name Brendan was mentioned in our house when I was growing up it meant him.

It was a *privilege* to hear you on the radio last week, he continued. I know it's a difficult time for the ol' fella. But I told him both he and your mother should be very proud of you, Gerard.

Thank God the rain is heavy, it'll disguise my tears, I thought as he squeezed my shoulder.

Thank you for saying so. It's good to hear it, I said as I looked at him. We said our goodbyes and I headed off in the rain.

Take care of yourself, young fella, he called after me.

★ ★ ★

I skipped the Galway leg of the Quilt tour and spoke at the opening ceremony in Limerick. The Quilt tour ended in Belfast on February 13th 1991. About forty people travelled from Dublin by coach. It was an emotional affair. Friendships had been built up during the tour. Different people from different backgrounds sharing a common purpose. The pooling of their grief. I knew, when the tour was over, that few of the friendships would endure. Their focus would disappear. Inevitable.

We stood around in a circle at the Belfast venue. Flanking the Quilts. Hands clasped. People were sobbing. People were invited to break from the circle, go to the mike at the top of the room, and say what they wanted, or needed, to say. I found the idea of speaking difficult. Part of me wanted to say nothing. But this was an ending. I had to say something.

I'd waited for seven years for the opportunity to express my grief for Paul, I told the group as I thanked the tour organisers for giving me the chance to do that. I could now get on with the rest of my life, I added.

God, you're difficult to get my arms around, John, the man standing next to me said as people embraced at the end of the ceremony. You're so big, he added.

My tears turned to laughter.

Clare and Rachel, the two tour coordinators and I travelled back to Dublin that evening ahead of the Dublin contingent. It was a relief to get away from the crowd. On the way we discussed our idea of setting up a group to develop HIV education and information. I decided that I'd stay on in Ireland and help them.

Clare and Rachel had met with hostility from certain quarters when they planned the Quilt tour based in the offices of the then Dublin AIDS Alliance. People thought of them as Trinity graduates, middle-class. I knew that they were two efficient women who got the job done. The Quilt tour could never have happened without them. They stuck with the project throughout all the flak.

* * *

It was February fourteenth. I was waiting for *him* to call.

Hello, I said answering the phone. It was just after seven o'clock.

Hello, Ger. I'm going to be late. I'm stuck in Kildare. Do you mind if we get a take-out and go to my place? he asked. Is that okay?

Sure. That'll be fine, I said.

He picked me up about an hour-and-a-half later. I'd bought him a chocolate heart for Valentine's day. He gave me a joint.

* * *

Rachel came up with the name AIDSWISE one morning over coffee. It was perfect. We'd arranged, with all the agencies working in the voluntary and statutory field of HIV in Dublin, to discuss our plans for the education initiative. Clare, Rachel and I walked into a meeting we'd called with representatives from the different organisations housed within Dublin AIDS Alliance.

Not a smooth meeting. Feathers were ruffled and egos were upset by our intended education venture. We were pilloried. People said we wanted to cut across the work they were doing. They also mentioned our privileged positions. They felt threatened.

As a HIV positive man I feel you're exploiting us, a gay man said campily.

Political correctness dictated that you couldn't argue with someone who was *directly infected*. The prevailing wisdom didn't allow room for those of us who were *merely* affected by the epidemic. It was a nonsense. We made as many diplomatic noises as we could and left.

Later we discovered that the same *man* who had received large amounts of money from an AIDS crisis fund, and had even counselled other people, who were HIV positive, as an expert by experience, was not, after all, HIV positive himself. It was he, in fact, who was exploiting people who were HIV positive! Such gall.

Clare, Rachel and I planned that we'd concentrate on areas that other groups were not covering. The joke of it all was that there was then, and still is, now, more than enough work for everyone to do. The idea that work was being duplicated was ludicrous.

Clare and Rachel decided that they'd had enough bickering and in-fighting. They would take six months out to reconsider their commitment to the work. It was a well-earned rest. During the Quilt, they had plugged away and even got Dr Rory O'Hanlon, the then Minister for Health to visit, unofficially, the Quilt.

The Minister hadn't, as it were, embraced AIDS at this point. People were appalled when two *activists*, one lesbian and one gay, verbally abused the Minister. They heckled him and called him *Dr Death* as the Minister walked around the exhibition. The Minister left abruptly. Months of careful work spent encouraging the Minister to understand went down the drain.

I carried on and developed AIDSWISE.

★ ★ ★

I went to Spain with *him* that Easter. We drove through the mountains north of Barcelona and spent three days in that city before coming home. The relationship was perfect but we hardly ever had sex. I walked into the bathroom one evening before going to Spain and came back with a box of condoms. Fear was palpable on his face.

We can't fuck, he said.

Why not? I asked.

I'm scared, he said.

Don't worry. It's fine, I said. There's more than one way to skin a rabbit.

But it wasn't fine.

Why do we have so little sex? I asked over dinner one evening in Barcelona.

Is it a problem? he asked as he looked across the candlelit table.

That's what I'm trying to find out, I replied.

We sat silently and continued to eat our meal.

I don't know if I'm involved with you for the right reasons, he said a few moments later.

What are the reasons you're involved with me? I asked raising my eyes slowly to his.

He paused.

I think, but I'm not sure, that I'm with you because I feel you'll take care of me when I, if, I get ill, he said. You won't be afraid.

Carry on, I gestured with my open palm as I raised the wine glass to my lips. You've got my full attention.

I'm not sure if that's why I'm with you or whether it's not.

He didn't say *or whether I love you*, I noticed.

What are you thinking? he asked.

I'm thinking that you better sort out why you're with me, I said.

We went on eating in silence.

What are you thinking now? he asked a few minutes later.

That you'd better not fuck me around, I said.

We finished our meal and left the restaurant.

Don't make me work too hard at this, I said on the street as we waited for a taxi.

I won't make you work too hard, he said. He squeezed my hand as we climbed into a taxi.

The next morning I went to see the Mies van der Rohe Pavilion. It's exquisitely tranquil there. I sat and watched the water reflect on the roof of the building and felt that my world had fallen apart. I loved *him*.

Afterwards I climbed the hill and watched the construction work on the Olympic Stadium. That afternoon I went to see the Gaudi buildings. We had great sex that night and on the last two days in Barcelona. The honeymoon is over, I thought as we flew back to London.

It was the beginning of the end. We got on well after the trip. The sex continued, sporadically. It had its highpoints. But, he dropped a bombshell one evening.

I don't desire you, he said. It was a Sunday.

I died an instant death.

We walked to the shop later that evening and I began to cry.

I can't help it, I said. I love you.

That's the tragedy of love, he said. One person always feels more than the other.

Time will help, he offered as I leaned my head back into a hedge and cried.

Perhaps, I said. But what happens when the pain creeps up later on, I muttered. It's just as painful as always.

I find you very attractive now, he said. The pain on your face makes you look so vulnerable.

So I have to throw my strength away, or spend the rest of my life crying, I blurted.

Wait there, he said. I'll go across to the shop. I'll be back in a few minutes.

I stood there and wondered if my life was falling to pieces. I realised it wasn't. But, that didn't make the moment any easier. I went home the next morning.

Nobody has the right to tell anyone they don't desire them. It's the cruellest thing you can say to someone who loves you.

The relationship trundled on for the next couple of months. We continued to see each other.

He was upset when I spoke of our "alleged" relationship.

Make no mistake about it, Ger, he said. We are definitely having a meaningful relationship.

But it had died by the following November. I stopped wanting him about a half-year later. We've stayed good friends. He's one of the better people God put into shoe leather, as my mother would put it.

* * *

My involvement with AIDSWISE continued. It was an education in itself. I found myself through the work. The anger and pain I felt about Paul's death was put to positive use. It's weird to learn that you've found yourself because of your worst experience. Valuable, yes. But, a high price to pay.

Chapter Twelve

It was frustrating. I knew what I wanted to say. I'd even worked out how to work a fax machine. And I'd researched the names and numbers of good journalists. But, I couldn't write a bloody press release. One that did the job well. I drafted one after another to no avail as I cursed the fact that investigative journalism doesn't flourish in Ireland. Most media stories are manufactured.

What? Why? How? Where? When? These are the basics. If your information answers these simple questions you're on to a winner. Kay came to my rescue.

Do it again, she encouraged. You're almost there. Remember journalists are busy people. If you give them something that tells a story, is well written and is verifiable they'll love you.

That is how my relationship with the media started. Awareness of AIDS had to be kept in the public eye. This was an important AIDSWISE strategy. To keep the debate alive. Newspapers and radio stations were vitally important if this was to be achieved. As were TV programmes.

Yes that's good, Kay said as I showed her my final attempt at a press release. Don't forget to put in your phone number so they can call you if they've got any questions.

Will do, I said smiling. Where would I be without you.

You can pay me in kind, she said. Buy me a pint later.

Deal, I said as we laughed.

AIDSWISE was about to launch an AIDS and Language Fact Sheet for journalists and a safer sex poster that targeted gay men. I climbed on my bicycle with posters and fact sheets in my back-pack and delivered them to all the newspapers and to RTE. I then faxed copies of the press release to all the news editors of the national daily papers and to the news desk in RTE.

It was August 1991. The Summer was hot and sunny. I went to a training session at Markievicz swimming-pool.

I parked the bike in the hallway when I got home. The phone rang.

Hello, I answered as I noticed the red light flashing on the answer machine.

Can I speak to Ger Philpott please? she said.

Speaking, I replied.

Hello, Ger, my name is Mary Wilson. I'm a researcher on Morning Ireland.

Hi, Mary, I said. What can I do for you?

Ger, we got the press release and the poster and fact sheet. They're very well produced, she said.

Thank you, I said.

Can you tell me a bit about AIDSWISE?

Its purpose is to provide targeted information about AIDS. It grew out of the Quilt tour.

Yes I remember. It was in the Mansion House earlier this year, she said.

There's a dearth of information about AIDS in Ireland, I continued. Especially on the prevention side.

What's different about AIDSWISE from other groups? she asked about ten minutes later.

AIDSWISE looks at HIV in a structured way and plans strategically, I said.

Ger, would you be able to come into RTE tomorrow morning to chat to us on air about the fact sheet and the poster? she interrupted.

Sure, I'll be happy to do that.

Do you have a car?

No I don't, I said.

We'll send a taxi for you, she said. What's the address?

Palmerston Park, I answered.

The taxi will pick you up at ten past eight in the morning, Ger, she said. Thank you for your time.

Not at all, I said. Goodbye, Mary.

I slept badly that night. I got up at seven the next morning. I was anxious as I waited for the taxi. This is a great place to live, I thought as I sat on the frontsteps of the house. The dew glistened in the hot morning sun. I was sub-letting the flat from a friend who had gone abroad for a month. The flat I'd found wasn't available until mid-September. The taxi pulled up outside the gate.

David Hanly's voice is familiar to any radio news-junkie's ear. So is his style of interview. The prospect of being interrogated by him doesn't fill me with joy, I thought. The temperature of the sun was already up.

It's going to be another scorcher today, the taxi driver said as we drove through the gates at RTE.

It's going to be a hot one all right, I said as I got out of the car. Thanks.

The adrenalin was pumping and my armpits poured like taps. David Hanly did interview me. And I wasn't tongue-tied.

You were very good, my mother told me later when she rang. What was David Hanly like?, she asked. He was definitely on your side.

He was a gentleman as you'd say yourself, Mum.

I'm chuffed with all the good reports from the neighbours, Ger, she said. Keep up the good work, love.

Thanks.

Take care, boy. I love you.

Bye, Mum. I love you too.

* * *

Hello, Ger, Ingrid Miley here from RTE's *Today Tonight* programme, she said.

Hi, Ingrid, I said.

We were wondering if we could do an interview with you for tonight's programme? she asked.

Sure, I said. Where do you want to do it?

We could come to your place if that's okay, she said.

That's no problem, I said.

Where are you? she asked. This is a Dublin 6 number isn't it? We'll be round within the hour, she said, when I gave her the address.

I ran what I wanted to say over in my head as I tried to stay calm. The doorbell rang.

Hi, Ingrid, I said when I opened the door.

Ger, she said as she shook my hand. Her handshake was firm.

The crew came in after her and set up the camera and lights as Ingrid and I chatted about the interview.

You'll be fine, she reassured me as she sensed my nervousness.

What an exciting job, I thought as they busied themselves with the preparations.

Thank you, Ger, that was great, she said when the interview was over. We'll go back now and check that this is okay, she said. Would you be available later just in case there were any problems with the camera? she asked as she turned towards me at the door.

You mean to do it again?

Yes. But I don't want to mess up your plans, she said.

No that's okay. I'll give you the number of where I'll be later, I said.

Ger, it's Ingrid, she said when I answered the phone. I hadn't gone out yet.

Is the interview okay? I asked.

Yes. Perfect, she said. I've just spoken to the producer of the programme. Ger, we'd liked it so much we want you to do the interview again live on tonight's programme, she added. Can you come into studio about eight-thirty?

Sure, I said as I drew a deep breath.

Do you know where television reception is?

Is that the same place for *Morning Ireland*?

The very place, she said.

Okay. See you later then, I said.

Thanks, Ger. See you at eight-thirty.

Shit. Live television, I thought. What have I done?

Emily, it's Ger, I said.

I thought the voice sounded familiar, she joked. Are you okay? You sound a bit off, she added.

Sorry for phoning when the News is on but I'm in a panic, I said.

What's up, she asked. Concern in her voice.

I've just agreed to do an interview with *Today Tonight*, I said. Live.

Terrific, she said. What are you wearing?

We'd met for the first time a few months earlier. She was speaking at a lecture organised for Gay Pride. An impending change was expected in the *1861 Offences Against the Person Act* which criminalised homosexual acts between men. She was a breath of fresh air as she cut through the wholesomeness of the affair. The faces of the gay politicos, who had organised the event, fell when she dropped the bombshell that there would be no change in the law for the foreseeable future.

She was aware of her effect and I found that entertaining. She was amused when I congratulated the organisers for inviting a panel of *heterosexuals* to tell gay men and women what life in post-gay-law-reform-Ireland would be like for them. We swapped phone numbers at the end of the lecture and haven't looked back since.

I didn't think you owned a shirt and tie, she said. Sounds very smart.

What am I going to do?

You'll be fine, she said. Hold up your left hand.

What? I said. This is no time for jokes.

Relax, she said. You'll need a bloody valium at the rate you're going on. When you get in they'll take you to make-up. They'll give you a jar if you want. But better stick to the Ballygowan. You'll enjoy it. Live TV is a great buzz.

Okay, I feel calmer already, I said as I looked at my left hand. We laughed.

When you get in to the studio, sit down. Relax. Breathe deeply. Before the camera rolls put your left hand on the desk in front of you. Put your right hand on top of it and keep them that way throughout the interview.

Why?

If you don't they'll fly all over the bloomin place, she answered.

Yes boss, I said jokingly.

Anything else? I asked.

Yes, she said. This is your big moment. On the flagship

current affairs programme. Knock 'em dead.

Who else is on? she asked.

Yes. Walsh.The National AIDS Coordinator, I answered.

Keep it polite, she said. Don't interrupt. You'll want to be asked back again.

Okay. Thanks a million, I said.

You're doing great stuff, she said. I'm proud o ye boiy, she added in a mock Cork accent.

* * *

On August 29th 1991 both Jimmy Walsh, the National AIDS Coordinator and I discussed AIDS in the presence of Brian Farrell.

It was a homosexual disease initially and then it got into the drug-abuser. And from the drug-abuser. They were the bridge to the heterosexuals. So it wasn't a heterosexual disease in '84/'85. I've been dealing with AIDS since '82 . . . We've concentrated on a school programme. Because I believe that that's where you should begin. With your schoolchildren. To let them know what AIDS is all about.

So said Doctor Walsh in his opening remarks on the programme.

For the record, Dail reports show that in a reply to a question the Minister for Education Mary O'Rourke said that *no specific guidelines have been issued by my Department regarding the education of pupils on the danger of AIDS*. It was April 8th 1987.

* * *

The *Evening Herald*'s TV columnist had the following to say about Dr Walsh's performance the next day:

The Government's new AIDS package will promote celibacy and fidelity, a line that Dr Walsh was pushing heavily. If you're moral, it won't happen to you, was the general tone of his argument.

People ask if anything ever changes in this country, and there, in two seconds of television, was the answer. Asked how people could be shocked into changing their ways he said:

I believe in fear. We haven't approached this in a hard enough way.

It seems Dr Walsh would like us to return to the days of puritanism.

★ ★ ★

The information programme Doctor Walsh spoke about on *Today Tonight* became available in schools in 1990. For someone who had been dealing with AIDS since 1982, Ireland's National AIDS Coordinator's, and presumably the Department of Health's, commitment to the enlightenment of the nation's schoolchildren was a *late* starter.

The so called *bridge* to heterosexuals may, or may not, have been from drug-users. Dr Walsh's theory was questionable epidemiology. But what is certain is that the route of transmission was paved by government inaction.

Dr Walsh also excelled himself that evening with his reference to homosexual behaviour and AIDS.

I believe in fear . . . it worked in AIDS already. You saw the way gays in the mid eighties suddenly changed their lifestyles. This is because they were looking at people dying . . .

It is true that some gay men, around the world, changed their sexual behaviour because of AIDS. That also happened in Ireland. With some gay men. For a while. At the time of Dr Walsh's comments, the Department of Health had done nothing to deal with the AIDS problem in the gay community. Despite the fact that a detailed report from Gay Health Action spelling out exactly what was going on was available to them. Dr Walsh's comment was cynical and showed officialdom's contemptuous view of gay lives. His words of wisdom revealed a multitude. It highlighted the fact that the people responsible for our (public) health saw fit to allow the deaths of our lovers and friends to act as a means of health education. The bastards have blood on their hands. This scornful attitude is what allowed a representative of the Department of Health, at a European Commission AIDS advisory committee level, to describe the voluntary AIDS sector in Ireland as being run by *a shower of homosexuals*.

I asked officials in the Health Promotion Unit (HPU) why, at that time, no action had been taken to inform gay men about safer sex practices.

Because it's against the law, they replied. We can't be seen to encourage illegal sexual activity.

What are you doing to change the law, I asked. Given that there is a Government commitment to do so.

The response was silence.

This is the same Department of Health who had, at this point in time, sanctioned the distribution of clean syringes to intravenous drug-users to stop the spread of HIV infection in Health Board run needle exchanges.

Can someone explain why one type of *illegal activity* was encouraged and another was not? I know the answer lies in homophobia.

* * *

Twenty-two friends of mine have died from AIDS in the past two years. There's a sense of revisiting my grief for Paul with each new bereavement. But this pain isn't just mine. Dublin's only crematorium is the latest venue for get-togethers. These rendezvous are happening too often. I look around at those gathered to bid farewell to loved ones and wonder who will be the next to depart. It'll be the same faces, the same sadness and loss. But with a different person in the coffin as it moves on the short conveyor belt through the velvet drapes. This scene punctuates our loss.

I'm envious of these ceremonies. And I think of the difference eleven years have made to the hollow ceremony that marked Paul's death. As I sit in the crematorium I think of *before and after* the now familiar theme. I wish that Paul never died. But I cope. I am a survivor.

★ ★ ★

Dr Walsh and his colleagues who thought little of gay lives got it wrong. Gay men didn't change their sexual behaviour out of fear because they saw their friends die. This is an offensive, thinly veiled excuse to allow homophobes off the hook for allowing the level of HIV infection in gay men in Ireland to rise unchecked.

The literature on HIV prevention was full, at this time, of articles about the uselessness of fear as a health education tool. Why did the man who was brought back from retirement to front the Department of Health's response to AIDS contradict this on national television? Did the officials who worked with him not keep him briefed? It would appear that the Department of Health were, permanently, *out to lunch* when it came to HIV prevention.

The gay men who campaigned for safer sex did so out of a concern for each other. And the knowledge that no one else would do it for us. Certainly not the Department of Health and our elected representatives. There was no political will to deal with matters of a homosexual nature. Gay men died, and will continue to die, as a direct result of this official negligence.

* * *

I wrote the following article for *The Irish Times* of Monday November 30th 1992. I channelled the anger I felt about AIDS in Ireland into the article. My anger has to do with the fact that many of my contemporaries, the people one would normally expect to be around in one's old age, will be dead when I'm old. There will be a big gap in my circle of friends when I'm old. This isn't natural.

I include the article and subsequent correspondence, a reply from the Minister for Health, Dr John O'Connell and a right of reply from me, which appeared later in the same newspaper.

Today, the eve of World AIDS Day, 41 people are corralled together in the separation unit of Mountjoy Prison simply because they are HIV positive. This enforced segregation is symptomatic not of a balanced medical judgement but of a wilfully inadequate response to AIDS. Arguably, it was because those initially affected by this disease were members of discriminated minorities that serious Government action was not forthcoming here.

The names of many politicians will be prominent in the history of AIDS in Ireland. It contains a veritable cast of procrastinators, distinguished because they framed issues politically rather than in the context of public health. This is to all our detriment. The outrageous price of their Hamlet complex has already been paid with 133 lives. Tragically, the final toll has not yet been tallied, with conservative estimates currently placing the level of HIV infection between 3,000 and 5,000. The ultimate cost will indeed be high.

This is not just about numbers. Numbers never reflect the isolation, despair and frustration of what it is to be affected by HIV infection. My friends, and others, who live with this reality are angry when they hear the Government repeatedly talk about surveillance strategies to get a fuller picture of HIV.

We all *know* this problem exists. By 1987 practically every European country had a comprehensive programme in place.

Let the record show that we have no Government-funded national HIV prevention programme. This official, ostrich-like response has manifestly resulted in minuscule prevention work while prioritising care and management issues. Lip service to safer sex advocacy is undermined by over-emphasing abstinence. In the absence of a cultural tradition that recognises the concept of sexual health and wellbeing, it is extremely difficult to approach the issue of HIV prevention. It means that marginalised groups are being ignored and effectively left to die. Nowhere is this better demonstrated than with gay men.

The World Health Organisation, in its "Health for All" policy document, recommends abolishing repressive legislation on sexual orientation. Four years ago, the Government gave an undertaking, to the Court of Human Rights, to decriminalise homosexuality. This has not yet happened. Regrettably, at the expense of gay men's lives.

As homosexuality is proscribed by law, the Government does not provide safer sex information for gay men, or anyone else. Gay men have unsafe sex because no one is telling us how not to. Why does the vision that allows the Government to provide needle exchange for IV drug use, also proscribed by law, not translate into HIV preventative strategies for other target groups? The Government may yet be sued for criminal negligence in this regard.

This year an unpublished survey conducted by the EHB revealed that 67 per cent of gay men reported having unprotected sex in the previous 12 months. Based on these findings, a long overdue clinic was established by the EHB in Dublin this Autumn – it operates at the AIDS Resource Centre at 19 Haddington Road from 7.00 – 9.00pm each Tuesday. In 1989 a study given to Government by the organisation Gay Health Action revealed similar findings. Despite this no action was taken. This three year period of Government inaction has, undoubtedly, led to gay men becoming HIV positive. Currently, gay men represent 33 per cent of AIDS related deaths here and, last year, reported HIV infection in gay men increased by 21 per cent.

Let the record show that the Government has only provided 10 hours of targeted HIV services for gay men in this State.

Significantly, heterosexual reported HIV infection increased by 28 per cent last year. This may cast a ray of hope on the bleak horizon of HIV prevention. Now that HIV is affecting the wider community (read non-gay and non-injecting drug user) more frank discussion on the role of condoms in preventing sexual transmission of HIV is inevitable. This will be a welcome development;

however, for some, too little, too late. In the inevitable rush to belatedly give this information it would be inexcusable if focused strategies addressing the needs of *all* groups were not provided.

Those who could have made a difference but did not, may be of the opinion that being HIV positive is a calamity one brought on oneself. For the record, blame does not enter into this equation. Being HIV positive has to do with bad luck. Bad luck to have been in the wrong place at the wrong time. Bad luck to have lived in a time when those charged with responsibility for public health had little courage and less vision.

I often wonder how they will sleep when they hear of a loved one being HIV positive.

I read the following letter in *The Irish Times* the morning I was to give a talk to 300 students at a private Business College in Dublin. I was early and went to the canteen for coffee. I bought the newspaper and read through it while I waited. I was gobsmacked. It's not every day you have a Government Minister's signature on a letter written about you in a national newspaper.

Sir,

I refer to the Viewpoint article (November 30th) in which Ger Philpott of AIDSWISE has expressed his view about the Government strategy on AIDS/HIV.

At the outset, let me say that I am pleased that Mr Philpott has indicated his satisfaction with key elements of this strategy, which relate to the care and management of those who have the disease and those who have contracted the infection and the measures which are in place to monitor the spread of HIV through comprehensive

HIV surveillance programmes.

He has been mistakenly critical, however, of our programmes aimed at preventing the infection and has used particularly strong language in so doing. It is important, therefore, to set the record straight regarding the consistent and orderly development by the statutory sector of preventative programmes and services aimed at preventing non-infected persons from the disease and those who are infected from transmitting the infection further. These initiatives can be summarised briefly as follows.

On primary prevention, the Department of Health has been operating AIDS/HIV information programmes aimed at the general public, at specific groups and at health professionals, since the mid-1980s. In this context, over 500,000 copies of the leaflet "AIDS – The Facts" have been distributed to the general public and several mass media campaigns have been implemented.

The Department of Education have developed an AIDS resource pack for use in second-level schools. The Health (Family Planning) Acts were amended to allow for the wider availability of condoms, in some cases free of charge.

On secondary prevention, risk reduction services, such as needle-exchange, methadone and condoms, backed up by one-to-one counselling are available in primary care facilities; Outreach programmes aimed at at-risk groups such as intravenous drug users, gay men and prostitutes are in place; State funding to the voluntary sector was increased significantly to facilitate the implementation of secondary prevention services.

I have also put in place a structure through which the Government AIDS strategy can be developed and implemented on an inter-sectoral basis, involving the statutory and voluntary sectors. Central to this is the National AIDS Strategy Committee, of which I am chairperson, and which has a significant membership from the voluntary sector.

So, far from being "ostrich-like" as Mr Philpott alleges, it is clear that the Government has been innovative and responsive to the evolving AIDS/HIV problem. In addition, we have not been judgemental, as Mr Philpott also alleges, and I think it is a pity that he is not as understanding as his colleagues in the voluntary sector are to the difficulties and complexities which all of us face, if we are to deal efficiently, effectively and compassionately with this major public health problem.

> Yours, etc.,
> (Dr) John O'Connell,
> Minister for Health
> Dublin 2.

I phoned Official X in the Department of Health to discuss the letter.

He told me that my article wasn't well received in the Department. He told me that he'd considered me to be a person he could work with. I told him that I was prepared to work with him. He said that I wasn't playing ball properly. He told me that he wrote the letter. That John O'Connell had signed it. And that if I responded to the letter it would only cause me trouble.

My response to the letter was published in *The Irish Times* on December 23rd 1992:

Sir,

Re Dr John O'Connell's response (letters, December

7th) to my Viewpoint article (November 29th). It was not, and would never be my intention to gloss over the crucially valuable work of my colleagues in other voluntary and statutory agencies. For anyone to infer otherwise would simply be incorrect.

My viewpoint, as expressed, put on record the irrefutable fact that since the beginning of this epidemic the needs of gay men and others, particularly in relation to HIV prevention, have been sadly neglected by successive Irish governments. This situation has changed somewhat, but only since early autumn of this year. Nevertheless, Dr O'Connell's response failed to address any of the questions raised in my article.

In April the National AIDS Strategy Committee's (NASC) report, chaired by Dr O'Connell, had the following to say on HIV prevention: "The provision of information in and of itself will not prevent the spread of HIV . . . this (should be) accompanied by a wide variety of other strategies". So much for the distribution of 500,000 copies of a leaflet.

The NASC report recommended the amendment of legislation to allow for the sale of condoms from vending machines. Dr O'Connell's family-planning legislation fell far short of this mark.

The NASC report continued: "Public awareness campaigns, community based prevention . . . initiatives and improved infection control procedures . . . should raise awareness about the disease, how the infection is spread and how the risk of infection can be eliminated". Bearing this in mind, the Government-sponsored World AIDs Day print media publicity campaign's failure to refer to condoms scarcely fulfils a commitment to primary prevention. It certainly did not live up to the

NASC recommendations, and in so doing wasted in the region of £60,000. This could have extended considerably HIV prevention work with gay men, amongst other badly needed community-based initiatives.

My understanding of what needs to be done on HIV prevention is borne of my personal experience of the tragedy – and loss – of a partner and too many gay friends, and others. It tells me that it is high time we called a spade a shovel in this country and stopped being so defensive about what is not being done.

Yours, etc.,
Ger Philpott
Dublin 4.

I presumed X meant that AIDSWISE wouldn't get Department funding. X also informed me that an amount of £10,000 pledged to AIDSWISE was no longer forthcoming because Albert Reynolds had made a Christmas gift of £1 million pounds to the Vincent de Paul. All spare cash within the various Departments was gathered up to contribute to this and as a result X said he had no money to give out. But I learned that other AIDS groups, promised money by X at that time, *did* receive their cash.

Chapter Thirteen

Spring 1983.

Declan Flynn lived alone in a bedsit on the northside of Dublin. I didn't know him. But I knew his kind of isolation. The fear of revealing his sexuality. Of being found out. The paranoia. The denial.

He went to Fairview Park, nearby his home, one evening in August 1982. The park was used by gay men as a cruising spot. They met there to have sex. For fun. For escape. For human contact. To lose themselves. And to find themselves in the comfort of strangers. There are several such venues in Dublin. And in most cities and towns throughout Ireland. Their whereabouts well-known *secrets* in gay circles.

A band of bored youths also went there in the evenings for fun. Dissatisfied kids – hormonal time-bombs. They also knew about the park after dark.

Let's beat up the faggots!

Great fun. Deadly fun, as it happened, that night in August 1982. The marauding gang of five thugs savagely beat Declan Flynn and left him for dead in Fairview Park.

Declan Flynn was like every other gay man in any of Ireland's cruising spots that night. Every night. He was defenceless. His only crime was to go to a place where he could express his sexuality.

Gay men cruise because they are forced out into the cold by society's prejudice. For some it's a necessity. For others it's a pastime. And for more again a compulsion.

The five juveniles were caught. They pleaded guilty to killing Declan Flynn. Found guilty and convicted, by Justice Gannon, in the Spring of 1983. They were given suspended sentences. Allowed to go free.

The decision handed down by Justice Gannon sent out a loud and clear message. The lives of gay people are expendable. Worthless.

The ruling provoked public outrage. A mass demonstration was held in Dublin to protest against the leniency of the sentences. People of all denominations, creeds, political affiliations and sexual persuasions united to express their horror at the decision.

I was in Cork at this time. I wasn't in the mood for going to Dublin.

A short time later, one of the five youths who killed Declan Flynn was convicted of another offence. He stole a handbag. He was sent to prison for two years. Again by Justice Gannon. The young man was too young to go to jail when he killed Declan Flynn. He was old enough to go to prison when he stole the handbag. But wasn't there *any* correctional facility available to which he could have been sent when his gang killed Declan Flynn?

It's disgraceful, if not downright bizarre, that it can be thought right to remove a young offender from the streets because he stole a handbag and not because he killed a man. A gay man.

Justice for all, my ass!

* * *

Summer 1990.

When I lived in San Francisco the debate about HIV prevention, among the politically active, focused on where it had gone wrong. On how it could be improved.

In the rush to provide much needed information on how not to get AIDS at the beginning of the epidemic not enough attention was given to the effectiveness of messages. People were back to unprotected sex. And the level of reported HIV infection was on the rise again. It was 1990 and the idea of relapse emerged.

Concern concentrated on how to convince people that sex without condoms was like russian roulette. To get them to practice safer sex. And stick to it.

Studies showed that people who always practice safer sex were those whose close friends had a positive attitude towards it. Peer education emerged as a possible solution. Energy and resources were put into the development of programmes where specific groups would design and implement education for themselves.

* * *

The bus climbed over the hill in Noe Valley. The straight run down to the Castro – a gay neighbourhood in San Francisco – at the bottom was like a roller-coaster ride. Jonathan and I were going to Cafe Flores for breakfast.

Hey look at the crowds across from the Seven-Eleven, I said at the stop before ours.

It's the Rubbermen stand, Jonathan said. They're doing a safer sex day.

Let's get off for a look, I said.

We crossed the street and joined the party atmosphere. Music played and people strolled past the information stands.

I suppose you're interested in the literature? Jonathan asked.

Naturally, I said laughing. Just like everyone else.

The Rubbermen were icons. A group of divine men who promoted safer sex. The gorgeous, sexy men volunteered for this imaginative safer sex promotion initiative. They dressed in rubber capes and wore masks, adding fun when they zapped the bars to give out condoms and information on safer sex. They were in civvies today – cut-off jeans and white singlets – the Castro uniform. They were chosen for their looks and personalities. And most of them had *yards* of personality. It was the currency of gay San Francisco. That and the tanned, toned muscular bodies.

Ger, this is Rod, Jonathan said.

Hello, I said smiling. It was a black Rubberman. I couldn't believe he called himself *Rod*. Jonathan and he kissed.

So you've been hanging out in the Pendulum, Rod said as he looked me up and down.

We all laughed. The Pendulum was a gay bar where black men who liked white men and vice-versa hung out in the Castro.

Not really, Jonathan said with a belly-laugh. We met at the Box – a disco.

So who's Rod? I asked as we made our way through the stands.

People were more interested in looking at the Rubbermen than the leaflets.

An old friend, Jonathan said, a grin from ear to ear.

Slut, I teased. Isn't it outrageous?

What? said Jonathan.

That he calls himself Rod, I replied. He laughed.

Believe me, it is, Jonathan said, innuendo in his voice.

We laughed as we crossed Market Street to the restaurant.

How long have the Rubbermen being going? I asked over breakfast which was now brunch.

A while, Jonathan said. They *hit* different places each night. The venues are the worst-kept secrets. So the bars are full of admirers waiting for their arrival.

I can see why, I said.

They walk through the bars and clubs to great applause and excitement. It's a real party, he said.

I can just imagine this happening in Dublin, I thought. Where would you get the good-looking men in the first place?

* * *

Summer 1993.

If Roger Casement was canonised Ireland's first gay saint he would, doubtless, bestow honorary status on the likes of Mary O'Rourke and Maire Geoghegan-Quinn. But they'd trot *far* behind our president, Mary Robinson. President Robinson signed into law the decriminalisation of homosexual acts on July 7th 1993. She brought a symbolic end to the twenty-year-long campaign for gay law reform in the Republic. Earlier Mary Robinson represented David Norris in his fight for homosexual reform.

Maire Geoghegan-Quinn, when Minister for Justice, did what no man before her would do. She decriminalised homosexuality. She didn't have the same difficulties in doing this as her male predecessors did. Another woman, the Minister for State at the Department of Labour and Enterprise, Mary O'Rourke, introduced visionary legislation in 1993. Her Unfair Dismissals (Amendment) Act 1993 made discrimination in the workplace on the grounds of sexual orientation illegal. This was another area of male procrastination in the past.

Lucky for Irish lesbians and gay men, indeed for the whole country, that we joined the Common Market, as it was then known. Most, if not all, of the social changes we've seen in this country happened because of Europe.

David Norris appealed the Irish Supreme Court's decision not to change the Victorian 1861 Offences Against the Person Act, in the Court of Human Justice in Strasbourg. This law had criminalised, among other things, sexual activity between males. The European Court ordered that Ireland's repressive laws about homosexuality should be changed. The Irish Government agreed to do that. But they dragged the leg. Albert Reynolds said once that homosexual reform was at the bottom of his agenda. But that was before he went into coalition with Labour in 1992.

The law was eventually changed in 1993. Seventeen is now the age of sexual consent for heterosexuals and homosexuals alike.

Law reform put the lesbian and gay communities on *terra firma*. A heterosexual friend pointed out that, while it represented a huge achievement, it was only one small step. How right he was. There is still a great deal of work to be done. Homosexuality is still anathema to most people in this country – even to many gay people themselves. How do you get people to accept the idea of men having sex with men, women having sex with women, and encourage people to come out? When Irish society doesn't accept that people have sex with each other. Period.

If gay people camp out on Irish society's doorstep waiting for the climate to change, they'll be there until Charles Haughey joins the Labour party.

We mustn't make victims of ourselves. Heterosexuals aren't the enemy. Yes, I know. Family Solidarity and Co. But they are no more *just* heterosexuals than Maggie Thatcher is *just* a woman. Sometimes the real villains are gay themselves. They sleep with you by night. Keep you invisible by day. They're the architects, bar managers, company executives, doctors, married men, media people, politicians, solicitors and teachers . . . They don't give a damn about our oppression because they've got their piece of the pie, and they got it by living a lie. Of course, people are entitled to keep their private lives private. But don't expect the rest of the world not to notice what you're really saying.

* * *

Summer 1993.

What are you doing this evening, Ger? my friend Ann asked when she telephoned.

I thought I might get an early night, I replied. Why?

A few of us are going to a gig in the Rock Garden. Would you like to come?

I'd love to, I said. I've never been. Hmm. It's Thursday. I guess I'll catch up on sleep at the weekend.

Great, she said. We're meeting in Hogan's for a jar at eight.

See you there, I said and hung up.

The pub was comfortably crowded. It was the height of Summer. The time when Irish people wear less clothes. To show off their brown bodies. Their sexiness.

Hello, Ger what are you having? she asked as she made her way to the bar. We'll have one more before we head off?

A bottle of Heineken, thank you, I said. My arrival made up the party of six.

Where did you park?

Dame Court, I said. Outside Fifi's – a gay nightclub. We finished our drinks and headed for the gig. We were in good form.

What's the new George like? asked Ann referring to the newly opened gay bar at the bottom of George's Street.

It's a big improvement. Much bigger and brighter, I said. Apart from being a bit like the dream kitchen you never wanted.

What do you mean?

It's full of hideous oak panelling. I replied. And a ridiculous nude hanging on the wall! But I'd give it seven out of ten.

The gig was good. It was a while since I'd been at a live music venue. I made a mental note to go more often.

What's it like to be legal, Philpott? a friend asked as we danced. She meant the decriminalisation of homosexual sex.

It's a difficult one, I shouted over the loud music.

I remember when I was in University. Involved with gay politics. Somebody said it would never happen in our lifetime. But it did.

All I can think of is that the argument that we're illegal no longer holds, I said. But I don't think the problems are over yet.

I said goodbye to my friends around one o'clock. I made my way to my car. On the way I decide to check out Fifi's.

Steamer. Arse-hole bandit, the voices shouted as I walked out of the alley between Dame Street and Dame Court.

I turned. A smile on my face. I thought it was some friends teasing. It wasn't. I froze on the spot. There isn't anyone on Dame Court, I thought. Five working-class youths stood about ten paces away from me. I won't be able to run back down the alley. I won't be able to make it to my car.

Don't show them you're afraid, I told myself as I stood tall. Two I can manage, at a push. Five is out of the question. Shit! They'll make mincemeat of me, I thought. I clutched my car keys in my hands. I clenched my fist. Tightly. I stuck the metal part of one key out between the ring and middle finger of my right hand. This will do one, maybe two. A kick will get another, I thought.

The streets aren't safe with the likes of you, they shouted as they stepped towards me.

I don't know what you're worried about boys, I said. You're so fucking ugly no one would bother with you.

I'd heard about harassment on the streets. My women friends often spoke about it. I even knew gay people who'd been beaten up. Hadn't these delinquents heard about law reform?

I found myself walking towards them. Anger erupted inside me.

Shouldn't you young fellas be at home in bed, I said. Christ, What are you doing? I asked myself.

The three younger ones ran off towards Georges Street. The remaining two – they were about sixteen – changed their stances. They were less menacing. I'd called their bluff. I turned and walked slowly toward my car. Would they jump me from behind?

Fuck it, I said when I got to the car. I want to beat the shit out of them. I walked to Fifi's door. Opposite my parked car. I rang the doorbell and went inside when the door opened. I walked quickly through the upstairs bar. Then I went downstairs to the dance-floor. I saw him. Someone I knew.

Would you like to beat the shit out of a couple of thugs? I've just been harassed by five young fellas, I said.

Where? said Chris.

Outside the fucking door, I said.

Calm down, he said. Come on, I'll buy you a drink.

Thanks.

Don't leave on your own, he advised as he made his way back to the dancefloor. I'll walk you to your car.

Homophobic bastards, I thought as I drove home.

* * *

Spring 1992.

Why don't you sit next to me at dinner this evening? she suggested as we left the bar.

She worked for the Commission. We were at a conference in Luxembourg. The place was called Club Cinq. There were twenty delegates – invited from nine different member states. It was January 1992.

Do you know Official Y? she asked, referring to a man I knew in Ireland.

We were now seated at the dining-table. She chose french onion soup to start. I had carpaccio.

I've met him, I replied. Why?

He's not gay-friendly.

Why do you say that? I asked. Partly annoyed by the English superiority which looked down on backward Ireland. Partly amused by her statement of the obvious.

Well, I met him at a group committee meeting a few weeks ago, she said. I asked him, over coffee, what the state of play with the voluntary AIDS sector in Ireland was.

And? I asked.

I was stunned by his response, she said. He said, it's run by *a shower of homosexuals*.

It figures, I said. That's what we have to put up with. They're still ignoring gay men in Ireland. So Official Y's a homophobe, I thought the next day on my flight back. I was spending the night in Paris.

But he's not the real slippery one, I thought. He's only a rookie.

* * *

Winter 1991.

I think we've spent enough time on this matter, Official X said from the opposite end of the table. Lines of Suits flanked each side.

There's a principle involved here, I said. If we don't put people with HIV at the centre of the debate, it's a nonsense.

It was the final planning meeting for the Sharing the Challenge Conference. AIDS Liaison Forum (ALF), the monthly meeting of statutory and voluntary sector workers on AIDS, were organising the conference with the Department of Health.

The plan was that the Minister, Rory O'Hanlon would stand beside a man with HIV infection. Publicly. Important symbol. Official X, on behalf of the Department, had agreed to that. We went to the last planning meeting for the conference and found that the programme was changed. Without consultation. A great way to share a challenge!

I was angry. The Suits were silent.

We'll be having coffee soon, X said. We can press on then. There're a lot of items on the agenda.

But it's important that this is sorted out, I said. You always agreed that the Minister would speak in the same slot as the person with HIV, I said.

I noticed the dandruff on X's collar and shoulders as the door opened. Coffee was brought in. People pushed back from their chairs. I felt that some of the Suits were annoyed. But they said nothing. I realised they wouldn't speak against the official programme. I wanted to shout. I didn't.

You're just like your father, the little voice in my head said. Tenacious. Sticking to the principle.

You grow up promising yourself you'll be different from your parents. Only to find one day, that you're the same.

That's not a bad thing, I thought. And I smiled to myself.

The Department's plan had sandwiched another speaker, Jimmy Walsh, the National AIDS Coordinator, between the Minister and the man with HIV. And a break for a photo-call for the Minister before Jimmy spoke. Significant distance.

You're a tough negotiator, Jimmy said as I stood beside him.

We were looking out the window of the ninth floor of Hawkins House. A monstrosity of a building. We could see the matt green river Liffey. The *Irish Press* offices on the bank below us. Liberty Hall on the far side. The sound of the Dart trains audible as they crossed the city, on the railway bridge that spanned the river.

Would you be prepared to let the man with HIV speak

before you? I asked. I wanted, needed, to see Rory O'Hanlon and the man with HIV together.

I've no problem with that, Jimmy replied. See what comes up at the meeting. Suggest that I allow the man with HIV speak before me. I'll agree.

Thank you, I said

It's a relatively simple thing to do, he said as he cleared his throat. I don't know why they're making such a fuss.

Meanwhile Official X was talking in a corner of the room with Fred, an ALF representative. Fred worked for a health board. As the meeting started again Fred beckoned me to one side.

You'd better let this drop, he said. They're getting annoyed.

I've found a compromise, I said enthusiastically. Jimmy Walsh has agreed to speak *after* the man with HIV so that O'Hanlon and the guy with HIV can stand together. I'll suggest this when the meeting re-starts.

Did you ask him to do this?

Yes. Just now, I replied.

That's great, he said as he looked at the floor.

We sat at our places. I fixed my tie. I was wearing my TV clothes. I looked benignly at Official X who was sitting at the opposite end of the table.

I'm anxious to push on, he said as he glanced at his watch. He then looked at Fred.

I think the programme that you've suggested is satisfactory, said Fred.

I couldn't believe what I heard. I'd just told him about the compromise that I'd reached with Jimmy Walsh. But Fred wasn't going to budge from the plan he'd agreed with Official X. Jimmy Walsh said nothing.

Great, Official X said. We'll move on then.

The voices around the table were fuzzy. Fred sold out. He wasn't going to rock the boat.

No progress will be made with AIDS as long as people with vested interests – such as their careers – are in the pockets of the policy makers.

You're a bollocks, I told Fred later. We were in Mulligans, for a pint, after the meeting. I can't believe you did that.

What else could I do? Fred laughed his high-pitched laugh.

You can stop putting yourself forward for delegations to the Department if you're not prepared to change the status quo, I said.

I left the pub and cycled home.

* * *

Winter 1991.

Mary O'Rourke was the Minister for Health who addressed the Conference. A recent Cabinet reshuffle had moved her from the Education to the Health portfolio. She was more dynamic than her predecessor, Rory O'Hanlon. He seemed ill at ease with AIDS.

The Minister spoke brightly about her establishment of a National AIDS Strategy Committee (NASC) to advise and formulate policy for handling AIDS in Ireland. She believed the conference would add considerably to that task. She looked forward to receiving the findings of the conference.

Well, so she would. It was late 1991.

But, so what. Better late than never.

This was the first initiative – by the voluntary sector –

to forge solid working relationships between the Department of Health and coal-face workers.

If only she'd been the Minister for Health when we were planning the conference. She wouldn't have refused to stand next to a man with HIV, I thought as he walked toward the podium.

He stumbled over his words. He was charming. A likeable character. He was a former drug-user. Who was now HIV positive. Nothing more liked than a repentant sinner. A prodigal son.

What do you think? she whispered as she leaned across her seat towards me.

She had been working with AIDS since the beginning. One of the best people in her field.

You know my feelings, I said. I admire him. But we don't need tokenism. We need a bloody good speaker who won't pull any punches.

You're right, she said. Another opportunity wasted.

Yeah. But try telling that to you-know-who, I said.

She laughed.

The you-know-who were the AIDS politicos. The people who had drifted through every cause there has ever been. But who found a niche and power in AIDS. The people who have never asked themselves the question: Do I need AIDS more than AIDS needs me? They do most of the shouting about exploitation. When, in fact, they themselves are the greatest manipulators of all.

Later a representative of Irish people with AIDS in Britain blew his cool.

The Chief Medical Officer and the National AIDS Coordinator were sitting on the stage. The guy from England wanted them to recognise that there was a problem for Irish people with AIDS who lived in England.

There are no figures for Irish people with AIDS in Britain, Jimmy Walsh said. Growled.

That doesn't mean that there aren't any, the guy from England said.

I don't have any figures to go on, said Walsh. The Chief Medical Officer agreed.

The audience shifted uncomfortably. They weren't happy with the way the Department of Health officials were dodging the issue. The officials continued with the glossy slide presentation.

Which one of you is the puppet and which of you pulls the strings? the man from England asked.

The presentation was like a boring puppet show. Did they care that the room was full of people, activists and statutory workers, who'd dealt with the problem of AIDS in Ireland from the beginning?

He's like a breath of fresh air, I thought. He wants us to admit there is a problem with Irish people who have AIDS in Britain. There wasn't much help for them at home. He dealt with them on a daily basis.

My job that morning was to pass the roving microphone around the hall. My sympathies were with the guy from the voluntary sector in England. He was far more honest than his Irish counterparts. The arrogance shown by Jimmy Walsh didn't help the situation. And the Department needed to be shaken out of its complacency.

Official X gave me the nod. He ran the index finger of his right hand quickly in front of his throat. He followed this, quickly, by cutting both hands, palms down, across each other, in front of his sternum. There was to be no more microphone for that particular speaker. I nodded. But I delayed. To give the guy from England a chance to finish what he had to say.

Speakers from the floor became annoyed with Jimmy Walsh's refusal to accept that his figures, the Department's figures, underestimated the real picture of AIDS for Irish people. At home and abroad. It looked as if things were going to get out of hand.

Perhaps I can explain the problem, I said, into the microphone. I was nervous. People turned to look at me.

People are *just* trying to point out that the problem is greater than the presentation suggests.

Official X nodded at me encouragingly. But he didn't know what I was going to say next.

For example, the slides we've just been shown tell us that no homosexual men died from AIDS in Ireland in 1983. But if you turn around and look at the Quilt displayed at the back of the hall. There is a panel to commemorate a man who died on the first of October 1983. He was a gay man. I made the panel. He was my lover. But he's not included in the official figures. The problem isn't as tidy as the figures might suggest. That's all that people want to be acknowledged.

Official X was no longer looking at me.

I felt as if I had ten heads.

★ ★ ★

The National AIDS Strategy Committee (NASC) was meant to put a structure on what had been, up to that point, a set of incoherent initiatives. Mary O'Rourke told the committee to focus on intravenous drug users and heterosexuals. She never mentioned gay people and there were no gay representatives on the committee. This *degaying* of AIDS, coupled with the heterosexual ethos of responses to AIDS, seriously narrowed the scope of NASC's work.

One of the four ALF representatives to NASC kept me informed of the committee's progress. She spoke about the frustration she felt. About what amounted to a slow process of education for the civil servant dominated committee.

I couldn't believe my ears, she told me. He asked me to explain to him what the difference between HIV and AIDS was. Ger, I'm talking about a medically qualified civil servant here. Can you believe that? Her face reddened as she spoke.

NASC's report was presented on the 13th of April 1992. Its recommendations form the foundation of the Government's policy on AIDS. Department of Health surveillance statistics on AIDS and HIV also inform the direction of AIDS policy. But this system of data collection is inherently flawed. It doesn't give an age, gender or regional breakdown of HIV infection data. So the profile of the epidemic is incomplete.

It doesn't make sense to base vitally necessary initiatives on inaccurate information.

The majority of the NASC recommendations implemented so far have had to do with drug use. The opening of community satellite clinics, for example, was heralded as the way forward. There was a suspicion that the centres were only for drug-users.

Drug-users were only getting attention because of AIDS.

Drug use was not getting the attention it deserved in its own right.

The Department of Health and the Eastern Health Board, who run the clinics, denied this. The clinics provided drug services in the mornings and HIV services in the afternoons. But now, at the beginning of 1995, the clinic's drug services have expanded into the afternoons. The sexually-transmitted-disease services that were initially provided have now been cut back.

And the clinics aren't *just* for drug-users?

I'm concerned that the community satellite clinics are over identified with drug-users, I said at a meeting between Department Officials and coal-face workers. This means that other people, gay men for example, won't go to the clinics.

But the clinics were intended for drug-users, Official Z, now deceased, said.

We all know that, I said. But it's the first time it's been said officially. And it isn't what the NASC report envisaged, I added.

It's always been what we'd planned, Z said.

* * *

Winter 1991.

I don't want to, she said.

But I really like you, he replied. I thought you liked me?

We watched them as they talked about whether they'd have sex or not. I looked at my colleague. We smiled. The others in the group couldn't take their eyes off them.

He moved closer to her and put his hand on her leg.

Let's try it for a while?

No, she said.

Everyone else is doing it, he said. Maybe we should break it off.

Stop I can't do it anymore, she said.

The group laughed. Brilliant, everyone agreed.

He was a she. And she was a he. We were doing a training exercise with the Ballymun peer education group. The role play required the players to swap gender and negotiate sex. The group would watch them and then discuss what happened. The idea was to get a better understanding of how people felt under pressure. It also gave an insight into how it felt to have the shoe on the other foot. It made for rivetting drama.

When I returned to Dublin in 1990 I put energy into researching the viability of peer education. AIDSWISE devised a model for working with young people on HIV prevention. But it also looked at the wider context of sexual health and reproduction. The project was developed with young people in Ballymun.

The preparatory work for the project in Ballymun began in November 1991. The plan was to work with a group of local adults. Then train a group of local teenagers. The idea was to produce a group of young people who could look after themselves in group work situations. And spread the word about safer sex.

* * *

Spring 1992.

Hello, Ger, she said.

Hi, how was Athens? I asked.

Great. Jesus, Philpott there's no getting away from you.

What do you mean? I asked mock concern in my voice. How can you say that?

We laughed.

I was in my hotel in Athens – she was presenting a paper at a Commission conference on AIDS in Greece, she said. I turned the telly on and went into the bathroom to run a bath. You know how addicted I am to CNN.

Yeah, get to the point, I said.

I couldn't believe what I heard, she said. They had a report of the peer education project being received by Mary Robinson. I dashed out of the bathroom. And there you all were lined up as you introduced the President to the group. It was fantastic, she added.

Brilliant, I said.

How did you wangle that? she asked.

I didn't. CNN called. They saw the RTE report on the visit to the Aras and picked it up for their roving magazine programme. The President had received the group from Ballymun to launch the project.

Ger, I just called to thank you for today, she said. She was one of the adult members of the project. The kids haven't stopped talking about it since. It's made their day. They can't believe that the President took the time to talk to them. They feel so important.

That's great, I said.

* * *

Summer 1992.

The annual international conference on AIDS was held in Amsterdam in 1992. One of the conference features was the inauguration of a recent research slot. The preliminary findings of the AIDSWISE peer education project was one of those chosen. It was great to get the imprimatur of the Harvard AIDS Foundation for the project.

I presented on the first day of the conference. A number of Irish delegates attended the conference. Only one, a doctor friend, came to the session. To lend me moral support.

Congratulations, Ger, she said afterwards. It's great to have an Irish project up there with the best from around the world. And about time what's not going on in Ireland is read into an official record somewhere.

She was talking about the official neglect of HIV prevention work I mentioned in my presentation.

It was frustrating. Neither the Department of Health nor the Eastern Health Board would row in behind the project. Requests for resources and personnel to develop the final stages of the project fell on deaf ears. As a result the project had to be scaled down.

* * *

Summer 1992.

Same slides. Different wives.

So goes the joke about the international AIDS conferences. About the romances that flourish during the week of the big event.

Dr Philpott, I enjoyed your paper, he said. I looked up.

Thank you, I said. It was great to be able to do it. I'm not a doctor.

We laughed. It was Tuesday, the morning after my presentation. We were travelling on the tram to the conference centre. His cut-off shirt showed his muscled arms off to good effect. His accent was American. A big turn on.

I'm sorry, he said.

Don't be, I replied.

My name's Keith. Here's our stop, he said as the crowd on the tram made their way to the door.

We looked at each other as we made our way across the plaza to the doorway of the centre.

Are you involved with peer education? I asked.

No, he said. I went to the presentation to see you.

Why? I mean . . . he looked at me and smiled. I blushed.

I picked up the press release about your paper in the press office, he said. I only noticed it because I remembered your name.

From where?

I saw it on your name badge at Sunday's reception.

I remembered that he smiled at me once or twice during the reception. I was there with Roisin Boyd. She covered the conference for her ground-breaking RTE radio series, Testing Positive.

Where are you from? I asked.

Seattle, he said. Are you here alone?

No, there's about fifteen people from Ireland here altogether, I replied.

I mean is your boyfriend with you?

No. I don't have one, I answered.

What's wrong with them in Ireland? he joked.

You're full of charm, I quipped.

Does it bother you?

Not at all, I said. Keep it up.

Want to go to a Wellcome presentation on AZT with me? I have to cover it for the magazine I work with.

I hesitated.

There'll be free food, he added.

Sure, I said.

We got there a few minutes after it began. I knew several people there. A friend, Jonathan, from London raised his eyes quizzically as I sat next to him.

Made a friend have you? he whispered. His gorgeous smile full across his face.

We met on the tram, I said cutting him off

Really? His tone camp.

This morning, I said.

Do you want to meet up later? Keith asked as the seminar ended. We could have dinner, he added. I looked at him for a while as I tossed an imaginary coin.

Why not, I said smiling.

Meet you at the message screen at six?

Look forward to it, I said as we went our separate ways.

* * *

Where would you like to eat? he asked. The heat was sweltering.

Let's go to somewhere we can sit outside, I said.

Great idea, he agreed.

It's much of a muchness, I said as we made our way through the busy streets. Let's go here, I said pointing to a nearby restaurant.

Would you like a drink? the waiter asked as we sat down.

A beer for me please, I said.

I'll have a coke, he said.

The food was typically Dutch. Typically Irish, really. Meat, veg, potatoes and gravy.

We chatted over dinner. Inconsequential stuff.

Can I ask you a personal question? he asked.

I though you'd never ask, I joked.

Are you HIV positive?

I looked at him for a moment.

No, I said. But I bet you are, I thought.

Is that a problem for you? I asked trying to lighten the situation.

No, he said. But it might be for you.

You're positive? I asked.

Not only that, he said. I've got AIDS.

How long have you been diagnosed?

Two years, he replied.

We discussed the state of his health. What his life in Seattle was like. Then we sat in silence as dusk fell.

Would you like to go to Aprils – a gay bar? he asked.

Let's do that, I said. Shit, I thought as I felt him withdraw into himself.

The bar was crowded and all the AIDS mafia from the conference were there. Amsterdam is full of beautiful men. We were surrounded by hunks. And the smell of marijuana filled the air.

Can I make an improper suggestion? I whispered into his ear.

Yes, he smiled.

Would you like to spend the evening with me?

Yes again, he replied.

We finished our drinks and headed for the tram. I'd sublet a flat from a man from West Cork for the week of the conference. He worked in a hotel bar in Amsterdam and had moved in with his boyfriend while I took his flat. Keith held my hand in the tram. We didn't talk. Just the odd meaningful glance at each other.

I was writing a complex script in my head. My confidence had been destroyed by the man I'd met at the opening of the Quilt in Dublin. Paul was also in there somewhere. It was important that Keith found me attractive. I needed to have sex with someone who had AIDS. That way I could lay a lot of ghosts to rest.

What would you like to drink, Keith? I asked as I opened a beer for myself.

I'll just have water, he said. To wash down my medication. He waved a vial of tablets before me.

What are they for? I asked.

They help me get a hard on, he said. I laughed.

You're joking?

I'm not. They work really well, he said. But I haven't used them with anyone yet. But they've been great for masturbation.

How do you mean? I asked.

I haven't had sex with anyone since my AIDS diagnosis.

Looks like we're both experimenting so, I said as I explained the complicated script in my head.

Should we talk about what's okay and what's not okay? he asked when we were in bed.

I just love American directness, I thought.

Let's see how it goes, I said as we kissed.

I had the most restful sleep I've had in ages, I thought when I woke up the next morning. Keith lay asleep beside me. We had to pace our sex. To allow him catch his breath. He tired easily. He stayed with me for the rest of the time I was in Amsterdam. We had great fun. We've chatted on the phone a few times since. I called him recently but his number is no longer connected.

★ ★ ★

Autumn 1992.

I was in Sweden in February doing research on a peer education project on HIV prevention for young people. The time, Harry Whelehan, then Attorney General, tried to injunct a fourteen year old girl, pregnant as a result of rape, from having an abortion in England. There'd also been another Cabinet reshuffle. Mary O'Rourke was no longer the Minister for Health. She was replaced by Dr John O'Connell.

John O'Connell tried to be all things to all men, especially his constituents. He abolished the post of National AIDS Coordinator the same week that the Harvard AIDS Foundation called for stronger national coordination of AIDS. O'Connell, unwittingly, I presume, made himself directly responsible for dealing with AIDS as a result of this action. His ministry was regarded as an interregnum. The result of this for AIDS policy was disastrous.

But it was entertaining to see his civil servants try to manage his merry dance. O'Connell was on *Today Tonight*, the then flagship current affairs programme on RTE one evening, talking about the proposed abortion legislation the Government had promised to introduce. I was meeting with officials from the Department of Health and the Minister the next day. As I walked from the lift into the corridor on the ninth floor of Hawkins House I saw O'Connell and Official X talking. X looked uneasy.

What did you think of last night's programme, O'Connell asked X.

X pushed past the Minister. He didn't answer his question.

Ger, good morning, he said. He walked towards me and grasped my hand. My arrival gave him a convenient opportunity to avoid answering the Minister.

I was never so glad to see anyone, X said as we walked into the conference room. I didn't know how to answer him, he added.

I laughed.

I saw the programme, I said. We looked at each other.

You know what I mean so, X said as he threw his eyes up to the ceiling.

X explained during the meeting that the Department would be in a position to make £10,000 available for the training phase of the peer education project. Money the project never got.

* * *

Spring 1993.

Gay saunas are popular with many men. Men who are gay and men who pretend they're not. Many of them married. It costs roughly about the same as a nightclub does. People know why they go there. They go there for anonymous sex.

Nice and neat.

Well, not really.

One of the uncertainties in the equation is why the owners of the places don't provide condoms. Another is why the customers put up with this.

You must go and see for yourself, a friend said. Get over your *sensibility* and check it out. They don't provide condoms.

I don't know, I said

Look on it as a field trip, he said. Some research.

Okay, I agreed.

I was intrigued by the idea of the sauna. We parked our cars and walked down the laneway together.

Even where it's located is seedy, I said.

We laughed.

A surveillance camera looked down on us. We rang the doorbell and stood inside the small hallway.

Hello, he said. That'll be seven-fifty each, he said as he

turned the guest book towards us.

I signed my name after my companion and handed over the dosh. He handed us locker keys and two small old towels.

He then buzzed us through another door. The place was tacky. It didn't smell very good either. We put our clothes in the lockers, wrapped ourselves in the worn towels and handed the keys back to the guy at the door.

The steam room, sauna and showers are in the back, my friend said. The cubicles and videos are upstairs.

We had a shower.

The showers can get quite busy sometimes too, my friend said as we went into the steam room.

It was empty. We sat inside for a while and heard the doorbell ring.

That'll be the after-pub crowd, announced my friend. Let's go upstairs and check out the videos.

There were a number of men undressing in the small locker-room near the spiral staircase as we went upstairs. Two older men sat drinking coffee at the coffee bar. They smoked cigarettes. I saw the sign pinned to the wall.

Condoms available at counter. Just ask.

It was handwritten on a faded piece of A4 paper.

I can't believe it, I said to my friend. Surely they can do better than that?

A fifth generation tape played on the TV screen. A close-up of two men fucking.

Original, isn't it? my friend quipped.

Very, I replied.

A couple of men, draped in small towels, sat in the wicker chairs. The dim lights accentuated by the bluish cigarette smoke.

These are the cubicles, my friend said.

The first door he tried to open was locked from the inside.

Busy, he said. Someone's got lucky.

The next door was open. Inside a small leatherette platform, the size of a single bed, filled the entire room. A shelf contained an ashtray and a bracket high up on the wall held a small TV. The porn video we saw on the screen in the hallway was also on view on this screen. Each cubicle is the same.

So this is where people have sex?

Yes, my friend said. And in the dark rooms around the place.

Why don't they put condoms in the cubicles?

Because they're too fucking mean, he replied

But the Eastern Health Board will provide them free, I said.

I bet not many people ask for them at the counter? my friend said.

This place reeks of denial, I said. Even though everyone knows what's going on very few would've the courage to go to the counter and ask for a condom.

They're minting it in here, he said. You'd think they'd have bowls of the things around the place.

At this stage we were back in the steam-room downstairs and the action was picking up.

Later we went upstairs again.

Come here, I want to show you something, my friend said.

We walked passed the men standing around watching the video. We went down a short corridor.

Look in here, my friend said. We were outside the door of the last cubicle in the dimly lit hallway.

Where?

At the side, he whispered. There's a gap.

Voyeur's delight, I said as I moved aside to let him see.

A group of men were having sex with each other. Two of whom were being fucked without condoms.

I've seen all I want to see for one evening, I said.

We made our way to the dressing-room, got dressed and left.

* * *

Irish gay men are used to accepting second best. I understand that not everyone can, or should, go around preaching doom and gloom about AIDS. But the Department of Health no longer publishes monthly figures on HIV infection. Because, it argues, AIDS should no longer be considered an epidemic. Without respect, given its track record on AIDS, how do we, how will we know if this is true? I was stunned to learn recently, from a friend in the advertising business, that the Department of Health spends more on oral hygiene than AIDS in some publications in the month of December. The month that AIDS awareness is supposed to be at its highest. Apparently the budget isn't there for pushing prevention messages. Why not?

* * *

Spring 1993.

I realised that I was ten minutes late as I locked my bike to a parking meter outside Fitzsers on Baggot Street. I was having lunch with a friend.

Hello, he said as he put the newspaper down. How are you?

226

Fine, thanks, I said. Sorry for being late.

Don't worry.

We ordered our food and caught up with each other's news. We hadn't seen each other for over a month. My lunch date was HIV positive. I wondered if I'd tell him about Denny, Paul's brother. He was ill and I'd been to see him in the hospital a few days earlier. It didn't look like he'd live much longer. He had AIDS. I was upset about this because it opened old wounds.

I've been to see Denny, I said.

How is he? I haven't seen him for a long time.

You know he's sick? He's not well, I said.

I didn't, he said.

Then there was an awkward pause. We looked at each other for a while. I needed to talk to someone about how I was feeling. I always listened to my lunch date when he wanted to talk about being HIV positive.

I realised he didn't want to talk about it.

What are you doing for the afternoon? he asked.

I must catch up on some writing, I said.

I've got another appointment, he said. I'll have to go now.

Okay, I said. Talk to you later.

Bye, he said. I'll drop your books in tomorrow.

Thanks, I said. Bye.

* * *

I put the phone down as the doorbell rang.

Hello, I said. It was my lunch date from the previous day.

I've brought your books back, he said.

Would you like coffee?

Love some, he replied as I put the kettle on.

Sit down, I said. It'll only be a minute.

We chatted while we waited. He fidgeted. He looked uncomfortable.

Ger, I've got something on my mind, he said. It's difficult but I think I'd better say it out.

What's up? I asked

I don't think our friendship is working out, he said.

I was dumbstruck.

How do you mean – not working out?

I don't think you've been supportive enough of me recently, he said. And yesterday in the restaurant when you told me about Denny. It was insensitive. You didn't care about my feelings.

I found it hard to focus and my stomach was churning. Is this is a joke? I thought. I looked at him for a few minutes. Silently.

I can't accept what you're saying, I said. If anyone has been supportive of you over the past couple of years, it's me.

He looked at me. What the fuck is his shrink doing with him? I wondered. I was angry but I controlled it. I tried to stay rational.

I realise that you might have had difficulty talking about him being sick, I said. But I needed to talk about how I was feeling.

He was silent.

Did it ever dawn on you that I might have been having difficulty with it? That I needed someone to talk to about it? I'm affected by this too you know.

I hadn't, he said.

This pisses me off, I said. You go on about being *insensitive*. Wrapped up in your own concerns. It's a bit

228

ironic don't you think?

He got up, put on his coat.

I find this very awkward, he said as he left.

I was livid when he'd gone.

He phoned about two weeks later to say that he'd been thinking about what I'd said and thought it was best to forget it. To leave it behind us. And move on.

How neat, I thought. How fucking convenient.

Denny died from AIDS in 1993.

* * *

Autumn 1993.

It wasn't until 1993 that an Irish Minister for Health had the balls to launch the first media campaign unequivocally urging people to practice safer sex and wear a condom. Brendan Howlin was responsible for this. He got a lot of praise for the campaign. It was seen to be significant. Indeed it was, but only in terms of what hadn't happened before. I went to the press conference for the launch of the campaign.

I entered the press room in Government Buildings. The auditorium filled up as we waited for the start. An official from the Department of Health informed the gathered crowd, journalists and people from the various AIDS organisations, that questions were to be asked by the media only. I looked around and recognised some journalists.

Hello, I said to a radio journalist from one of the Dublin-based independent stations. My name is Ger Philpott from AIDSWISE. Would you ask the Minister a question about the campaign for me?

What's the question?

Why he didn't target specific groups, like gay men? I asked

I can't, he replied.

I had similar responses from a number of other journalists. I sat down as the minister and the officials from the Department of Health took their seats. I noticed Nell McCafferty come into the room as the Minister was being introduced.

I made my way across to her.

Nell, my name is Ger Philpott.

Oh, aye. Hello, she said in her sing-song voice.

I explained the question I wanted her to ask the Minister.

Why don't you ask the question yourself? she asked as she looked at me.

Only the press are allowed to ask questions, I replied.

Who says?

They announced it before you came in.

Shite, she said. Isn't this a free country?

Obviously not here, I said as she threw her eyes to the ceiling.

Write down the question she said as she handed me a piece of paper.

I then went back to my seat on the far side of the room.

I'd like to ask a question, Nell said when the Minister had finished his presentation.

Go ahead, said Brendan Howlin.

I was delighted. She'd stick it to him, I thought.

I'm asking this question on behalf of Ger Philpott who's sitting over there. He tells me that he's not allowed to ask the question.

Thanks Nell, I thought.

He's such a shy fellow. He wouldn't be able to ask the question himself, he said sarcastically.

Minister, we were told by one of your officials that only the press were to ask questions. I'm very happy to ask the question myself.

The Minister's *uncoy* messages were based on fear. Generic messages of fear. But, eleven years into the epidemic the literature on HIV prevention stated clearly that messages of fear didn't work. Didn't any one tell the Minister this?

Why didn't you target gay men in the campaign? I asked.

I didn't wish to stigmatise any one group, he said.

Horse-shit, I thought.

But, Minister, the biggest increase in reported HIV infection was in gay men last year. A targeted message wouldn't have stigmatised gay men. It might save lives.

I think I've answered that question, he said. Any other questions? he asked; cutting me off.

Later no one would talk to me at the coffee reception. All of the people from the other organisations, the Department officials, they all avoided me. When I approached them they'd move off after a few moments. It was like the Emperor's new clothes.

Of course all the journalists wanted to interview me then. My argument received plenty of coverage that day on radio and the next day in the newspapers. That was great. But I was getting pissed off with my colleagues' lack of balls.

In essence nothing had changed. Gay men were still being ignored by officialdom's denial.

Is it any wonder that gay men themselves are missing the point?

Spring 1994.

Early in 1994, two gay men were beaten up by a group of drunken middle-class men at the top of the laneway where I was harassed in the Summer of 1993. The two men, a couple, had been out with some friends. Their drunken assailants approached them from the opposite direction and began to hassle them. It was obvious that they'd be violent. The couple made a dash for the door of the Central Hotel. The doors were being closed. They knocked at the door. A doorman opened the door slightly. The men asked for help. The doorman closed the door. Meanwhile, the drunks, who had run after the two, had now caught up with them. They beat them up systematically. And kicked them to the ground outside the hotel. People passed by. Didn't stop. Didn't help. When the attackers had had enough fun they went on their way. Laughing.

The doorman from the hotel then opened the door and brought the two beaten and bloody men inside the hotel. The gardai were called. They took statements from the two men and said there was nothing they could do.

* * *

Spring 1994.

I heard you on the radio the other day, she said.

I was having coffee with a friend who worked as a counsellor with people with AIDS.

You were very good, she said.

Yet again I was talking about the increase in HIV infection.

Yeah, I said dejectedly.

What's up? she asked.

Oh! You're going in to your counselling mode now I guess.

We laughed.

It's getting to be a bit of a media circus, I said. People will get fed up listening to me. The same voice all the time. They'll switch off.

You're an excellent spokesperson, she said.

I know that. But it's like round up the usual suspects. People need to hear new voices. We need new blood.

Yeah but there *ain't* nobody else out there, she said.

There must be, I said. I feel that as long as I'm the only one, people will sit back and allow me to do it. I don't want to be Mr AIDS, Ireland forever thank you very much, I said.

I know what you mean, she said. But if you go who'll carry on?

I don't know, I said. *Someone* will have to.

We won't hold our breath, she said as we ordered more coffee.

Last week I was going to visit a friend in hospital, I said. I knew he had AIDS but he'd never told people.

Oh yeah, I know who you mean, she said. We looked at each other knowingly. Glances didn't compromise confidentiality.

She had worked with most of the gay men who were HIV positive.

The phone rang as I was about to leave for the hospital, I continued. It was a mutual friend of the man I was going to visit and myself. Do you know what he said to me when I told her where I was going?

What? she said as she looked at me.

You'd better not he said, I told her. He'll be freaked

out because people will know what's wrong with him. They think of you as the *angel of death*.

* * *

Summer 1994.

The official response to the needs of gay men, in this epidemic, has been one of sad neglect. The level of new reported infections amongst gay and bisexual men increased by 18% for the twelve month period to August 1994.

What is the state doing about this?

Not enough.

Successive administrations have conveniently used the popular and misleading myth that *the gay community has been responsible. Gays have modified their sexual behaviour.* There is no evidence to support this.

Indeed there is evidence to shatter the myth.

Younger gay and bi-sexual men, off on their first sexual experiences, seem to be more vulnerable to infection. Generally speaking, they have sex with older men. Some of these older gay men believe that the younger inexperienced men haven't been exposed to HIV. The older men dislike using condoms. The younger gay men may not *know* about AIDS. Neither would they know anyone with HIV. Nor would they have the confidence, or the assertiveness, to insist that condoms are used. Bingo.

The rate of new infections has gone up in gay men in the under-25 years age group, throughout the developed world.

There is no age breakdown on these figures available in Ireland – why not, Minister?

There is no reason to believe that young, and not-so-young, Irish gay and bi-sexual men are practising safer sex.

Recently, I learned of two young gay men who discovered they were HIV positive. These men were normally vigilant of their sexual health. They had regular check-ups for sexually transmitted diseases at clinics.

It's now no longer possible to get these services at Eastern Health Board clinics. Why?

The two men also knew that they were HIV negative. For several years. They became HIV positive as a result of one *slip* so to speak. One evening, independent of each other, they both succumbed to the temptation of having sex without condoms.

Why did it happen to me? Or. Why have I survived? A labyrinth of subconscious thoughts. The unasked questions in the minds of gay men. Who have lived with AIDS for more than a decade.

There are many differences between HIV positive and negative men. But AIDS is unavoidable for all of us for the rest of our lives. If you are not HIV positive now, you live with uncertainty until you die. Especially when you add the guilt of survival. The enormous loss that HIV negative men live with. It can't be less difficult than having AIDS. This is complicated. To find a balance between hope and honesty, safety and abandon.

Because of the reputation of AIDS, the normal support structures aren't there for people with HIV. The comfort got from sexual – life-affirming – contact may not be there for people who are positive. Sex is difficult for people with HIV. So is telling someone you're HIV status. Positive or negative. How will they react? This is a daily anxiety for someone who is HIV positive.

In the past twelve years, gay men around the world

have developed safer sex education, social service and support programmes, to meet the immediate demands of the crisis. When this started we believed that the crisis would be temporary. Now, we accept that AIDS will be around much longer than first envisioned. This has profound affects on our strategies – political, medical, emotional and sexual – for the foreseeable future.

Our psyches are affected by this epidemic.

The imperative message of HIV prevention – to stay negative – ignores the needs of HIV positive men. The pure safer sex message does not work. Safer sex is a constantly moving target. We are less certain about how HIV is transmitted now that we were when we began. Oral sex used to be safe. Now it's not.

Often, when gay men are living out their sexual fantasies, they're putting themselves in the *here and now* as they escape the horrors and future of living with AIDS.

Safer sex doesn't recognise this. Instead we've created a rhetoric of what's right and wrong. It's between what's right and what's wrong that people are becoming HIV positive – ask the two young men.

We grieve for *before*. When the expression of our sexuality was carefree. Yet we live in the *after* era. The desire for sex without rubber. The acting out of our fantasy is potentially disastrous. The consequences of this – a new wave of the epidemic in gay men in the late nineties – is too horrific to contemplate.

We have to re-think living with AIDS. About how, why, where and when we have sex. Psychotherapy. The concepts of denial, displacement, projection and transference have a role in this.

It's high time the State demonstrated its appreciation for the valuable work done by gay men and women on

AIDS by following our example. At best, we can hope for realistic financial subventions from the State. It isn't advisable to hold your breath for the Government to introduce campaigns. The official neglect of gay men has and will continue, to be paid for with human life.

I don't know exactly how many friends have died since the beginning of the epidemic. I do know that the devastation of AIDS will continue unless we can stop the transmission of HIV.

Why are young gay and bisexual men having risky sex? Because it's exciting. Foolish. But exciting. The only reason I do safer sex *is* because it's safe. Not because it's fun. It's been around for too long. I'm *bored* with safer sex.

★ ★ ★

Winter 1994.

It was October 1994. I was at the premiere of *The Lion King*, a fund-raiser for Body Positive, the self-help group for people with HIV. I was blinded by the strobe lights in the hallway of Dublin Castle. It was past midnight. People were leaving. I was going to a party with my boyfriend and some other friends, at the Irish Film Centre and then on to Lillie's Bordello to join the premiere crowd.

Hang on a minute, I said. I've just seen someone I should say hello to.

Hurry up, they said as they walked under the awning leading to the State Apartments.

Hello. How are you? I said to W. He seemed drunk.

I don't think I should shake hands with you, he said.

Why not? I asked laughing.

Because I read what you said about me in *your press release*.

I don't know what you're talking about?

I got your press release, he said.

I looked at W as he staggered. And I thought it was only SPUC who kept files on people!

Which press release? I said. We issued one every month – until you stopped providing us with the statistics on HIV and AIDS.

The one about the international AIDS conference, he said.

Oh! That one I said disingenuously. If you have the press release you'll see that never mentioned your name.

W looked at me aggressively. I realised that he was very angry as well as very drunk. There was no point continuing the discussion.

W, I don't think we're going to get very far with this discussion right now, I said. I'll be happy to talk to you about it, or anything else, some other time. Goodnight.

I walked towards the door of the marble hallway.

You're a bollocks, W shouted. I've done more for AIDS than you or anyone else in this country!

That's a matter of opinion, I said as I turned back to face him at the door.

That's right, W said. That's my opinion and you can go fuck yourself. That's if people like you can get it up.

I laughed.

W, I think you shouldn't say much more, I said. You're showing your true colours. Go home. Sober up.

I crossed the courtyard to join my friends.

Did you hear all that? I asked.

Yeah, what was *all* that about? they asked.

Lucky man you didn't clock him one, one of the women in the party, a prominent journalist, said when I'd explained what had happened.

More satisfying, that I got under his skin, I said.

Consoling isn't it, she said. *That's* who's involved with AIDS policy in Ireland. God protect and help us, she added.

* * *

Autumn 1994.

AIDSWISE never got central Department of Health funding. The Health Promotion Unit have contributed small amounts (£10,500 in total) to some AIDSWISE projects since 1992: the initial research for the peer education project, a grief and bereavement training project for statutory and voluntary sector workers throughout Ireland and a film project.

AIDSWISE is the only body who puts pressure on the Department about AIDS. The other agencies, all in receipt of central Department funding, remain tight-lipped.

He who pays the piper calls the tune.

The monthly figures on HIV, made available by the Department of Health about AIDS, were used for this purpose by AIDSWISE. A yearly analysis of the figures was made. The percentage increases for each of the four identified risk groups – gay men, drug-users, heterosexuals and children born to at-risk mothers – were plotted. Stress was put on the increased rise in reported HIV infection. The rise was consistently greater in gay men and also in heterosexuals. We made appropriate comments to accompany the press releases. Colleagues who worked in the statutory sector would pass on information that they couldn't use. Because they had jobs to consider. AIDSWISE acted as a conduit for the flow of information. Through this strategy, AIDSWISE kept the debate on AIDS in Ireland alive. Vast amounts of well-informed column inches were generated. Newspapers, radio and television were cooperative. Nothing like a bit of media pressure to get the men upstairs to take notice. The boys downstairs – the Xs and Ys of officialdom – got off their arses and did a bit of work. The Department responded. So did the Eastern Health Board.

AIDSWISE also briefed TDs and Senators for debates and questions on AIDS in the Oireachtas. As a result of AIDSWISE lobbying plans have been put in train, and a budget also, I presume, to have Fiona Mulcahy, the AIDS consultant at St James Hospital run the sexually-transmitted disease services at the Eastern Health Board clinics in 1995. When in 1995 I don't know. This overworked consultant will now be responsible for the AIDS Unit at St James Hospital, the Eastern Health Board services and a new weekly clinic in Trinity College, Dublin.

Wouldn't it make more sense to appoint another consultant to take care of this excessive workload? This appointment was recommended by NASC.

These Eastern Health Board services stopped when Louise Pomeroy, the clinical director of the service, reluctantly resigned her post in 1993. Her terms of employment were a joke for a qualified consultant. She operated the services without any budgetary provision from the Eastern Health Board. The two year gap – since the services stopped (and will restart one hopes) – suggests how the statutory services respond to AIDS. AIDSWISE set an agenda.

But since August 1994 the Department of Health has refused to make monthly figures on AIDS available to AIDSWISE. Several newsprint, radio and TV journalists have also been refused access to this, public, information.

Could it be that the policy has been adopted by the Department to avoid being embarrassed in the media?

* * *

Spring 1995.

NASC is now trotted out as a convenient PR exercise when the Department is put under pressure about AIDS. A representative, independent task-force must be established – not one dominated by civil servants – to prioritise action on AIDS. The first duty of this body should be to force the Government to admit that it doesn't have a coherent policy for dealing with AIDS. At least for groups other than drug-users. Gay men, for example. Or heterosexuals. *Even*.

* * *

In a recent (January 1st 1995) *Sunday Tribune* feature on AIDS, Barry Desmond, who was the Minister for Health in Ireland in the early eighties, when a realistic response to AIDS would have made all the difference, said of his inaction:

> It was not for the want of trying. I was constantly requesting, demanding and seeking the budgetary provisions for it [information on AIDS] but it just wasn't forthcoming. There was a huge hostility at that time to any kind of liberal sexual morality.
>
> It was a ridiculous situation. You couldn't get condoms without a doctor's prescription. Homosexuality was illegal and any attempt to decriminalise it would have been political assassination. There was an extraordinary reluctance at the time to promote public health.

And who was responsible for the promotion of said public health, Minister?

Barry Desmond made a cock-up of the foundation of the Irish Government's response to AIDS. And he hanged himself in the article by trying to play the grand old man of politics from the lofty heights of Europe. But hasn't he played a blinder politically?

★ ★ ★

A medical expert said in the same *Sunday Tribune* (January 1st 1995) article that there are at least two thousand more people in Ireland who are HIV positive than indicated by the official figures. I've been saying that for a long time and so have other people. Nothing is being done about this. And the Department says there isn't an epidemic.

HIV infection is not rampant in Ireland. But it is increasing, consistently.

By an average of about 8% each year for the past four years.

It's important that the medical AIDS specialists working in Ireland put pressure on the powers that be to get a move on with AIDS. This doesn't just mean hospital beds and equipment. Attention must be given to prevention. You can't play politics all the time, doctors, not while lives are at risk. The crisis response to AIDS has to stop. So must the cynical way the Department of Health has dealt with gay men.

The problem with AIDS and HIV is going to get a lot worse before it gets better. It will never be solved from inside the status quo. There's no room for complacency.

Somebody had better do something about it.

In the words of the late American gay activist, Harvey Milk:

No more dreaming, the time has come to awake.